I0623184

STALKED

TERRIFYING TRUE CRIME STORIES

VOLUME 3

ETHAN HAYES

FREE REIGN

CONTENTS

INTRODUCTION

Every day, countless lives are shattered, invaded by an insidious force that lurks in the shadows—the haunting menace of stalking. It is an affliction that knows no boundaries, transcending age, gender, and social status. It preys upon the innocent, the unsuspecting, and the vulnerable, leaving its victims trapped in a web of fear, uncertainty, and anguish. These are their stories.

Welcome to *STALKED*, an intimate and compelling anthology that gives voice to the survivors, the brave souls who have endured the torment of stalking. Within the pages of this book, you will encounter a tapestry of firsthand accounts, each one a poignant testament to the indomitable human spirit and the harrowing reality of being pursued by obsession.

The narratives you will find here are unfiltered and uncensored, representing the diverse experiences of those who have lived through the darkest chapters of their lives. These individuals have chosen to break their silence, to offer their stories as a beacon of awareness, and to illuminate the haunting reality of stalking.

Through the pages you will bear witness to the psychological warfare waged by the obsessed—a dance of manipulation, intimidation, and violation. You will discover the trauma that seeps into every facet of life— the sleepless nights, the constant glances over shoulders, the shattered sense of security.

But this anthology is not just a collection of tales of suffering and despair. It is a testament to resilience, to the indomitable spirit that refuses to be silenced. These stories are a testament to the strength found in community, the support of loved ones, and the power of the human will to overcome even the darkest of adversaries.

As you delve into the pages of *STALKED*, prepare to embark on an emotional journey—a journey that will make you question the boundaries of personal safety, the fragility of our digital age, and the measures society must take to protect its most vulnerable.

By amplifying the voices of the survivors, this book seeks to dismantle the silence that often cloaks the reality of stalking. It serves as a call to action, urging society to confront this pervasive issue, to lend a compassionate ear to the victims, and to collectively work towards creating a world where stalking is not tolerated.

May *STALKED* shine a light into the darkest corners, instilling empathy and fostering a collective effort to eradicate the shadows that shroud the victims of stalking. Let us embark on this journey together, to listen, to learn, and to stand united against the pernicious force that is stalking.

According to the Stalking Resource Center, 7.5 million people deal with stalking each year, and 15 percent of women have experienced stalking victimization at some point during their lifetime in which they felt very fearful or believed that they or someone close to them would be harmed or killed. If you or someone you know needs help, please check out the Stalking Resource Center and if you need immediate assistance, the Victim Connect Helpline provides information and referrals for victims of all crime and can be reached at 855-4-VICTIM (855-484-2846).

CHAPTER 1

THE GREY HOODIE

IT WAS a night like any other at the library. As an arts major, I spent most evenings in a tucked away corner of the fifth-floor stacks, researching and reading for my literature classes. I loved ending my days enveloped by the smell of old books. It was calming. It was my major for a reason. At this point in my academic career most of the things I needed to study were in locked vaults or in the reference areas. That meant plenty of studying, plenty of hand cramps and lots of coffee. It became my nearly everyday schedule. That night, I was so engrossed in analyzing Middlemarch that I lost track of time. The librarian had to ask me to leave at closing. I gathered my heavy bag, thick with books, and headed out into the biting winter air. As I was leaving, I noted a man in a grey hoodie leaning over an open computer. I gave a small smile once we locked eyes and then went about my way.

As I walked the few blocks to my studio apartment, I couldn't shake the prickly feeling that I was being watched. But I was huffing and puffing already struggling with the sheer weight of my backpack and couldn't just whip around. I decided to stop and adjust my bag. As I was doing so, I glanced over my shoulder and caught a tall, bald man in a tattered gray hoodie ducking behind a tree. He clearly didn't want to be seen. My chest tightened and I quickened my pace. I thought to myself that I must be wrong that nothing like this had ever happened to me before. My palms began to sweat as I thought of routes to escape through. Out of the corner of my eye I could see him catching up to me. Maybe I forgot something, and he was just following me every where I'm going. Shaking my head, I knew this didn't make sense to me.

By the time I reached my street, I was sure he was following me. My mind raced. I didn't want this stranger to know where I lived. I needed to lose him. I turned the corner and abruptly changed course toward the more populated part of town. The streetlights comforted me. If I could just make it a few more blocks to the 24-hour diner, I could call my "roommate" to pick me up. I pulled out my phone and pretended to talk to someone, recounting my exact location. I knew if anything happened, the police could access my recording for evidence. I kept glancing back to see if he was still there. His hood obscured his face, but his hulking frame trailed half a block behind. Despite my speed in walking quickly, he was making a decent pace to catch up to me.

I darted into a few open businesses debating whether they could help me out or not but I didn't want to look like a crazy woman seeing things or worse ha, but he lurked across the street until I came back out. His persistence terrified me. My legs ached from the freezing wind and carrying 20 pounds of books. I was running out of ideas.

Then I spotted a group of teenagers gathered under a streetlamp at the skatepark. I hesitated, then made a beeline toward them. They eyed me warily as I approached. I worried that they wouldn't take me seriously or just thinking I was being dumb. But at that point I thought that a chance was better than no chance at all. I must've seemed so awkward in that moment but I was getting super desperate. I in my fear I could get passed my awkwardness.

"Hey, I'm so sorry to bother you guys," I said, my voice quivering. "There's a man following me. Could I hang with you for a few minutes so I can call the cops?"

They turned to look behind me and saw the hunched over man in a grey hoodie pretending to be on his phone just walking aimlessly around. I explained to them the situation and I just couldn't take it anymore. They turned to face him down. The man froze locking eyes with them and then went back to pretending to text on his phone. The kids nodded and made space for me in their circle. As nonchalantly as possible, I dialed 911. I remember stumbling out the words, "He's been trailing me since the library. I don't know what he wants, but he won't leave me alone." My hands shook as I gave the dispatcher our location. I wasn't certain whether it was the cold or not, but I couldn't stop shaking.

The group closed around me protectively until the police cars arrived, surrounding the man. Once he saw those flashing lights, He tried to flee but was quickly intercepted. The officer asked if I'd like to file a report back at the station. I declined, too exhausted, and over-whelmed to relive the experience again that night. I asked if I could do so later once, I got myself together. They were reluctant and frankly I couldn't blame them in the least. However, the most interesting of surprises came when the cops ran the man's ID and found he was a known predator wanted for stalking other women. Luckily he had already had a warrant for his arrest. When they searched through his effects, they found exactly what I had feared. A pocket full of zip ties and his back pocket with a Bowie knife. I shuddered, real-izing how much worse things could've been if I hadn't found help. I wondered what horrible plans this man had for me. What was going through his head when he decided to stalk me? No, I stopped myself in that very moment. I was going to spiral down to a dark spot if I wasn't careful and I had been through enough for the day.

The skateboarders waited with me until I got in a Lyft safely. As the car pulled away, I broke down sobbing. I was endlessly thankful for those strangers and their instinct to protect someone in need.

A few days later, after the terror had subsided, I returned to the skatepark with freshly baked cookies. The same group was there again. When they recognized me, their faces filled with concern. I know it was corny but I couldn't help myself there was no way I could thank them enough for standing by me.

"I just wanted to thank you all for the other night," I said. "Things could've ended so much worse if you hadn't been there. You really saved me."

I recounted the full story, from noticing his sinister gaze at the library to the cops apprehending him. They listened intently; happy they could help. I wished I had learned their names that night.

"You all are amazing," I said, handing the cookies to the guy who first offered me refuge in their circle. "If there's ever anything I can do to return the favor, please let me know."

They replied something along the lines of, "Don't

worry about it," he said. "Anyone would've done the same. We're just glad you're safe."

I left the park feeling a renewed sense of hope. My night could've ended tragically, but thanks to their selflessness, I could share my story and pass on the importance of looking out for one another. It was a lesson I'd never forget.

After the police apprehended my stalker, they informed me he was a known predator in the area. Over the past few months, multiple women had filed reports of being followed by a man matching his description. Just last week, he had attacked a barmaid walking home after her late shift. She managed to fight him off before he could rape her, but not before he left her badly beaten. Thanks to her description, the police were able to identify him as the serial stalker. He had prior convictions for assault and battery. This time the district attorney pushed for the maximum charges. He pleaded guilty to attempted rape, assault, and stalking charges, and was sentenced to 5-10 years in prison. Knowing he was off the streets brought me some peace of mind. But I was still rattled, constantly looking over my shoulder as I walked home alone from the library. I realized I needed to better protect myself.

I started taking self-defense classes at a nearby martial arts studio. The instructor taught me physical techniques to disable attackers if needed. But she also helped me become more aware of my surroundings and project confidence to avoid being targeted. I started asking campus security to escort me to my car at night. And I made sure to leave the library earlier before darkness fell. I avoided walking alone on side streets, sticking to well-lit main roads. While my sense of security was shaken, I refused to let fear control me. I took back my power over the situation. My nighttime habits have changed, but it comforts me knowing I can handle myself if I ever feel threatened again. The self-defense skills I've gained have helped me regain my confidence.

CHAPTER 2

UNPARANORMAL ACITIVITY

LAST NIGHT WAS one of the longest shifts I've worked in a while. As an ER nurse, I'm used to the chaos and stress of back-to-back trauma cases, but yesterday felt endless. By the time I clocked out at 11pm, I was utterly exhausted. All I wanted was to get home, take a hot shower and crash in my bed. But when I pulled into my driveway close to midnight, I was met with darkness. A power outage. Just great. I dragged myself out of the car and fumbled with my keys to unlock the front door. Inside, my little house was pitch black and eerily quiet. No humming of appliances or electronic devices, no ambient light creeping in through the windows. I felt along the wall for the flashlight I keep by the door for occasions like this, but my hand grasped at nothing. Of course. Blindly, I shuffled through the dark house, my eyes struggling to adjust. I made my way to the living room by memory and collapsed onto the couch, still wearing my blue hospital scrubs.

I briefly considered changing clothes, but decided it wasn't worth the effort of feeling around my room for pajamas in the dark. Exhaustion overtook me and I started dozing off right there on the lumpy couch. As I slipped into unconsciousness, the old house started making noises around me. The floorboards creaked, the walls popped and crackled. This was nothing new; the house often made these sounds as the temperature changed. Still, in my half-asleep state, the noises unnerved me. I realized I had left the front door unlocked in my haste to get inside earlier. What if someone was creeping around the dark house? My foggy, overtaxed mind started imagining an intruder taking advantage of the blackout. I strained my ears, listening for any sound out of the ordinary. But there was nothing beyond the usual groans of the aged structure. Eventually I dismissed my paranoia as sleep deprivation and allowed myself to stop fighting off unconsciousness. I'm not sure how long I was out before I jerked awake. Disoriented, it took me a second to remember why I was sleeping on the couch in the dark. Then I became aware of a new sensation...the feeling of being watched.

I held perfectly still, all my senses on high alert. My

eyes had adjusted well to the darkness by now, but I still could discern no shape or figure in the living room. Yet I couldn't escape the mounting dread that something was in there with me. The fine hairs on the back of my neck stood up and my heart started slamming against my ribs. Then I heard it - the distinct creak of a floorboard near the entrance to the living room. My head whipped towards the sound. I expected to see the shadowy outline of an intruder, but there was nothing. Just empty darkness. Then another creak emanated from the opposite side of the room, as if someone was deliberately lurking just outside my line of sight. My fear spiked into momentary panic and I leapt off the couch. "Who's there? I know you're in here!" I called out, trying to keep the tremors from my voice. No response except for deafening silence. I fumbled for my cell phone on the coffee table and turned on the flashlight. I swept the beam over every corner, every nook and cranny, looking for any sign of an intruder. But the room was empty. There was nowhere for someone to hide. But I knew what I heard. Those creaking footsteps were real. Wasn't it? Doubt started creeping in. Had I dreamt the sounds? Hallucinated them in my exhausted, stressed state? I hesitated, frozen in indecision, senses straining for the slightest indication I was not alone.

But the dark house remained silent. After what felt

like an eternity, the adrenaline rush subsided and I slowly lowered myself back onto the couch. I kept the cell phone flashlight trained towards the living room entrance as I laid down. Sleep was out of the question now; my nerves were too shaken. As I stared wide-eyed into the darkness, the shadows seemed to slowly shift and morph before my tired eyes. I shook my head and refocused, reminding myself it was just my imagination getting carried away. Nothing could hide for long in the beam of light from my phone. My mind started rationalizing what I thought I had heard. The house was old. It settled and groaned on its own at night, especially when rapid temperature changes occurred, like during a power outage. I was stressed and exhausted, it was late, and my senses were primed for alarm after the long and harrowing shift I'd just worked. There were no intruders or ghosts. Just stress and shadows playing tricks on my weary mind. But some primal, intuitive part of me remained tensed, unsure.

So, I laid there in the darkness until the first pale gray light of dawn seeped in through the windows. The power remained out, but daylight restored my rationality and courage. I no longer sensed a lurking presence. In the clear morning light, the bizarre events seemed like nothing more than the product of an overactive imagination fueled by fatigue. Still, I trusted my instincts enough to know something last night felt off. As I brewed coffee on the gas stovetop and prepared to face another day, I resolved to call my friend Martha in the evening. Martha runs a local paranormal investigation group part-time. If anyone could determine if my dark house harbored more than just creaky floorboards and moving shadows, it would be her team. Just to be safe, I would have Martha do a full workup of the place. At least then I could rest assured knowing my home held nothing more ominous than the echoes of a long nursing shift and an exhausted mind. I had to know for sure. Because the feeling that I was not alone in the darkness lingered in the back of my mind, as persistent as the unseen presence itself. I needed an answer, a rational explanation. Only then could I truly rest easy again.

After the strange events that happened during the blackout, I called my friend Martha the next evening as planned. Martha was more than happy to send her paranormal investigation team to my house later that week. Though I felt a bit silly asking her to investigate what was likely just the overactive imagination of an overtired mind, I knew I wouldn't rest easy until I had definitive proof, one way or another, that my old creaky house was not haunted. Martha arrived Thursday evening with her partner Simon and medium Evan in tow. I gave them a quick tour of the house and explained what happened the night of the blackout. They unpacked an array of equipment - EMF meters, infrared cameras, digital thermometers. Martha explained how each device worked, though most of it went over my head. I was no ghost hunter, just an ER nurse relying on science and logic to get me through this ordeal. For the next few hours, Martha, Simon, and Evan slowly worked their way through the house, taking readings and periodically calling out requests to the "spirits" to give them a sign.

The meters would occasionally light up or beep, which the team assured me meant they were detecting supernatural energy. I remained skeptical. Meanwhile, Evan wandered from room to room, eyes closed and palm extended, as if feeling for ghosts invisible to the rest of us. Finally, he shivered and opened his eyes. "There is a dark male presence here. Angry, parasitic - he's feeding off the fear and stress of the living inhabitant of this home." His gaze landed on me knowingly. I shifted, unnerved by Evan's showmanship and dire pronouncements. But Martha and Simon seemed to take the medium in earnest. If it would cleanse my home of this unseen presence, real or imagined, I was willing to go along with one of Evan's elaborate ceremonies. We scheduled a series of follow-up sessions to fully "purge the negative energy." A bit excessive, but I just wanted peace of mind again.

Over the next couple weeks, Evan and the paranormal team returned to perform various rituals, chants, and cleansings throughout the house. I observed Martha closely during these visits. Though she was focused on the tasks at hand, I started noticing little tells - a furrowed brow here, a tight smile there. Something about her demeanor seemed... off. I finally pulled Martha aside after one visit, under the guise of taking a cigarette break. Once outside, I turned to her and asked point blank, "Is everything okay? You seem uneasy lately when Evan is around." Martha hesitated before letting out a heavy sigh. "To be honest, I haven't been getting any legitimate meter readings during his visits. No temperature fluctuations, no EMF spikes. But I don't say anything because..." She trailed off uncertainly. "Because Evan is so confident in his psychic findings?" I guessed. Martha nodded. "I know you want answers, so I didn't want to undermine the process. But scientifically, we haven't found evidence of an actual haunting here. I think once this last visit with Evan is done, you'll be able to rest easy."

I trusted Martha's judgment completely. If her tools weren't picking up on paranormal activity, then whatever happened during the blackout must have been all in my head. Feeling relieved, I thanked Martha for her discretion and for humoring Evan until the end. She gave me a supportive hug, and we returned inside to finish the investigation. After the final visit, I saw the ghost hunters off feeling much lighter. That night I slept deeply and peacefully for the first time in weeks. The following few weeks were blissfully uneventful. No more creaks or shadows in the night. I was certain the stress of that night caused my mind to play tricks on me, nothing more. Then, four weeks later, I awoke in the darkness to a loud crashing sound downstairs. I grabbed my phone and leapt out of bed, pulse racing. As I crept down the stairs, the overhead lights suddenly flicked on, then off again. More crashing sounds emanated from the kitchen down the hall. Heart pounding, I ran to the kitchen and flipped on the light. Pots and pans were strewn across the floor, presumably the source of the noise. But what could have caused them to fall? My cat jumped onto the counter, knocking things over occasionally - but she was curled up on the couch, undisturbed. A chill went down my spine. Was I losing my mind?

These new incidents couldn't be written off as coincidence or imagination. Something was very wrong here. Terrified and confused, I called Martha for help. Within an hour she arrived with Simon and Evan. As we gathered in the living room, Evan's face was grave.

"The spirit is back," he proclaimed, "and angrier than ever. His energy permeates this space. He is too powerful for me to banish alone now. We must perform the Divine Rite ritual immediately."

Though apprehensive, I knew I had no choice but to

continue trusting Evan. Whatever was happening felt very real this time. The investigators spent the night performing elaborate chants and rituals in every room as I watched anxiously. Finally, as dawn broke, Evan declared the home had been cleansed. The spirit was gone. My shoulders sagged in relief and exhaustion. Martha and Simon packed up the equipment without a word while Evan communed with the "spirit world," assuring the ghost it could not return. I thanked them wearily as they left, this ordeal finally over. The paranormal occurrences stopped after that.

The debunker in me wondered if it was all some elaborate hoax Evan orchestrated somehow for money or fame. But I could come up with no rational explanation for the bizarre events I witnessed. Ultimately, it did not matter. My home was peaceful once again, the shadow lifted. I knew I should feel relieved. But a part of me wondered if I had just opened a doorway to something beyond understanding - something that might one day return.

For weeks after Evan's final ritual, my home remained peaceful and undisturbed. I took it as proof that whatever presence had lurked here was well and truly banished. Martha assured me that a negative entity powerful enough to resist Evan would have made itself known by now. My sleep was untroubled, my senses no longer assailed by anomalous noises or movements in the night. I allowed myself to believe that the ordeal was finally over for good. I fell back into my usual rhythms - long shifts at the hospital followed by blissfully normal nights at home. About a month after Evan's last visit, I left work early with a severe migraine.

I pulled up to my house, I noticed the lawn crew I hired was supposed to come today. Not wanting to block the driveway, I parked at the curb. As I gathered my things, the movement near the side of the house caught my eye. I glanced over to see the door of my crawl space swinging shut. For a split second, I saw a pale hand withdrawing back inside. I stood frozen in shock and disbelief. Had someone been hiding in my crawlspace this whole time? What little color remained drained from my face. Legs shaking, I stumbled back to my car and scrambled inside, locking the doors. With trembling hands, I called 911 and hysterically tried to explain what I saw. The operator dispatched a patrol car immediately. In what felt like an eternity but was probably only minutes, the police arrived. Two officers crept towards the crawlspace entrance: guns drawn. As I watched in paralyzing dread from the street, they cautiously opened the door.

One shone a flashlight inside while the other kept his gun aimed into the darkness. A startled exclamation rang out as a figure inside was illuminated. "Come out with your hands up!" the officer yelled.

Heart hammering, I watched as a filthy, disheveled man crawled out and stood up, raising his hands. When the man turned his face towards me, I gasped in stunned disbelief. It was Evan - the psychic medium. Shock rendered me speechless and motionless as the officers grabbed him.

Evan's eyes were wild as they met mine. "I can explain!" he kept shouting desperately as the police cuffed him and led him to the patrol car.

But no explanation could justify this - hiding in my home, invading the privacy I believed had been restored. Numb, I watched the car disappear down the street with Evan inside. The remaining officers conducted a search to determine if Evan had an accomplice.

Finding nothing, they took my statement and left, but not before showing me the disturbing makeshift living space Evan had created under the floorboards mere feet from where I slept. I stood in my driveway as the implications sank in. Evan had never been gifted. The paranormal events were staged, part of some warped plot to insinuate himself into my home and life. Revulsion shuddered through me at the violation. I couldn't spend one more night here knowing what Evan had done. Hands still shaking, I packed a bag and checked into a motel. The next day I informed my landlord and decided to break the lease. Within two weeks, I was in a new apartment across town. In the weeks that followed, I declined to visit or even drive by the house again. The thought of seeing that crawlspace made bile rise in my throat. Instead, I authorized a real estate agent to handle packing and selling the property so I could put the ordeal behind me. The police investigation revealed Evan had been living under the house for at least two weeks before I caught him that fateful afternoon.

He confessed to rigging the paranormal activity in some sick effort to ingratiate himself with me as a savior. The violation I felt was indescribable. Months later, Evan took a plea deal to avoid trial. Part of me wished I had my day in court to face him. But a larger part just wanted closure. The deal ensured he would be locked up for several years, unable to worm his way into more unsuspecting lives. For now, that would have to be enough. In the end, the only thing haunted about that house was my memory of the predator who hid himself in its depths. These days, living alone, I still feel twinges of lingering unease. But I try not to let the experience close me off or make me suspicious of human decency.

Whatever darkness lurked within Evan, there is far lighter in people worth trusting. And I never again live anywhere with a crawlspace. For all I know, it's an irrational fear. But it's a boundary I must have after coming so close to unwittingly sharing my home with true evil. What happened can't be changed. I can only keep moving forward and trust my instincts should shadows ever threaten to invade my life again. For they inevitably will try. But I am stronger now, having survived the darkness once already. I will not cower or flee. I will stand tall, cast light on their secrecy, and force them back to whichever hell they crawled out of. Where they can haunt me no more.

CHAPTER 3

420DELITE

I REMEMBER the first day I had signed up for TikTok. I thought, "why the heck not? See what's out there." Then after hours of scrolling I discovered I could do that. I loved dancing and connecting with people. When my TikTok dance videos first started going viral, I was ecstatic. After years of dutifully posting choreography tutorials and learning the latest viral moves, my follower count was finally exploding. I still remember the exhilarating rush I felt the day I hit 100k followers. Then 500k a week later. Soon I was gaining millions of new followers daily as my videos got shared around the app. Brand sponsorship offers came flooding into my inbox. I signed up with a top digital talent agency to help manage the influx. They negotiated deals with athleisure brands, makeup companies, even big-name soda, and snack corporations.

The money was unreal. At 22 years old, I was making over $10,000 for a single sponsored TikTok post. I rented a luxury apartment, filled my closet with designer clothes, and still had plenty left to invest. When the fame started going to my head, my agency recommended launching my own product line to stay grounded. I decided on a collection of cute, affordable yoga pants and sports bras. I used my newfound wealth to hire designers and manufacturers. I chose joyful, colorful prints that matched my bubbly personality.

My followers ate up the #OOTD shots of me dancing in my own yoga pants. The collection sold out within hours of launch. I rapidly expanded the line to meet demand. Next, I leveraged my lifelong dance experience to create "Get Fit with Me" style workout videos. I demonstrated easy-to-follow routines set to the latest pop hits. Followers flooded my comment sections expressing gratitude for the no-judgement approach. I made sure to tune out the diet culture noise and instead embrace body positivity. I ate I t up. My empowering message resonated with young women everywhere. I skyrocketed to 10 million loyal followers who felt like family. My dreams were coming true before my eyes.

Until the day @420delite entered the chat.

At first, it seemed totally normal. Just friendly comments about my yoga line and workout videos. I appreciated the positive vibes. But then 420delite's questions got...personal. They asked about my skincare routine and hair care products. I happily recommended my faves, sharing affiliate links to earn commission. When 420delite asked for a custom video demonstrating my skincare routine up close, I felt a twinge of unease. But my sponsor Bonita Cosmetics was thrilled at the publicity opportunity.

So late one night, after filming a new dance challenge, I propped up my phone in the harsh bathroom lights. Applying serums and creams, I captured close-ups of my bare skin glistening. It felt a little odd, but I figured it was just part of being an influencer.

420delite was ecstatic, commenting effusive praise and thanks. But their next request made my blood run cold.

> Your skin is divine! Can I come over sometime and experience its perfection in person?

Every hair on my body stood straight up, alarmed by the proposition. I figured 420delite was simply over-eager and meant no real harm. Gently, I replied that for privacy reasons that would not be possible. 420delite apologized for being too forward. They said they just got carried away in my beauty. I decided to give them one more chance. When 420delite asked about my hair routine next, I relaxed a bit. I posted a *"Get Ready with*

Me" video, carefully demonstrating my favorite hair products.

But the very next day, 420delite commented:

> Your hair looks so soft. Can I buy some strands?

I froze in disbelief, skin crawling. This had gone way too far. I knew I had to cut ties with this obsessed fan immediately, for my own safety. Who the hell asks a question like that? I tastefully declined. But decided that it was in my best interests to cut this person off. After I blocked 420delite, I thought that would be the end of my nightmare. How wrong I was. Over the next few weeks, burner accounts with random usernames started popping up in my comments and lives. At first there were a few inappropriate remarks here and there that I could easily delete and ignore. But then the harassment escalated. These accounts, surely all controlled by 420delite, started spewing vile, sexually explicit taunts. They threatened to find me and "teach me a lesson" for rejecting them. Why was I being punished for their terrible behavior? Then other content creators started making commentary about the ongoing drama.

I was mortified. I started censoring my lives in hopes of discouraging them, but they always found a way back in. The graphic language terrified me and could get me banned from TikTok if I didn't stay on top of deleting it.

After a month of constant bullying, I decided to take a break from social media entirely. My mental health was suffering. I was anxious to leave my apartment, worried 420delite might try to track me down in person. My hair and skin care sponsorships were put on pause. I stopped responding to brand partnership offers. My career felt like it was falling apart. I had worked so hard to get where was and it was going to pot.

After a few months of therapy and taking time for self-care, I finally felt ready to return. I decided to refresh my look with a dramatic hair change to mark my "come-back." I chopped off over 8 inches of hair, leaving me with a chic blunt bob. It was scary letting go of my long locks but felt symbolic of leaving the past behind. My fans were thrilled to have me back. I regained my momentum, partnering with new brands and returning to regular content creation. Thankfully, there was no more sign of 420delite.

One day, I decided to unbox gifts from my P.O. box on a live stream. As I tore open packages from sweet, thoughtful followers, my mood lifted.

That is, until I unwrapped an ominous black box. Inside, a Ziploc bag stuffed with strands of long brown hair. My heart dropped into my stomach like a stone. Hands shaking, I read the enclosed note:

Thanks for your hair! Took a while to

collect all the strands you so carelessly discarded, but it was worth it. I don't like your new cut. This style suits you better.

I nearly vomited right then and there. It all came rushing back - the fear, violation, torment I thought was behind me. 420delite had found a way back into my life once again. I somehow managed to maintain composure, thanking my viewers through gritted teeth before abruptly ending the stream. As soon as I was offline, I crumbled.

I became hysterical, hyperventilating with panic. I retched into the nearest wastebasket, choking up bile and tears simultaneously. That sick freak had been following me, collecting my discarded hair from salons, my apartment, who knows where else. This was no longer just online harassment - they were stalking me. With shaking hands, I called the police to report the disturbing package. But after explaining the situation, they informed me not much could be done legally. No direct threats had been made, nor had I been physically harmed. At most, they could make a note in case things continued to escalate. I felt helpless and alone.

I stayed locked inside for weeks afterward, terrified to go out in public. My online presence became sporadic as I constantly feared another attack. It felt like 420delite had already stolen so much from me. And they weren't finished yet. After the disturbing hair package, I became a prisoner in my own home. I was too terrified to leave my apartment, convinced 420delite was lurking right outside my door. My TikTok content suffered. I tried filming safe indoors, sticking to choreographed dances and beauty tutorials. But even that felt dangerous. One morning, I propped up my phone to film a new dance challenge. As I was perfecting my moves, I heard the apartment door creep open. My heart seized in my chest. I abandoned my phone and whirled around. A man slipped into my apartment, closing the door behind him.

"Hey there," he said casually. "I'm a big fan."

Every nerve in my body screamed to run, but I stood my ground. "Get out!" I yelled, my voice trembling. "I'm calling the cops."

As I stared down at the intruder, my eyes landed on his jacket - a brown leather vest with...fur trim? No. My stomach dropped. Not fur. It was hair. Long brown strands that I recognized instantly. Remnants from the sick package 420delite had sent me. Bile rose in my throat as I watched him gently stroke the hair collar, a disturbing smile forming on his lips.

"Don't worry," he purred. "I just came to give you a little trim..."

He took a step toward me, raising the scissors in his hand. Adrenaline flooded my veins. I lunged for the landline on my kitchen counter, slamming 911 and shrieking into the receiver. The man simply blinked at me, unfazed. Then without a word, he turned and left, shutting the front door softly behind him. I sagged to the floor, hyperventilating through panicked sobs. Moments later, police sirens wailed outside. Once I could form words, I directed the officers to my still-recording phone propped on the counter. We gathered around the screen as the scene replayed.

There was 420delite, as real as the hair vest adorning his shoulders. Video evidence of him breaking into my home. Terror washed over me again. But this time, it was coupled with relief. I had proof of his disturbing obsession. Justice would be served. As police examined the footage, an officer revealed that 420delite was a notorious stalker who targeted young influencers. But he always managed to evade charges due to lack of evidence. Not this time. The hair vest he so proudly flaunted on camera ensured an ironclad case. A search of his home uncovered a collection of...trophies. He wouldn't hurt anyone again.

In the following weeks, my anxiety remained high. I flinched at every stray sound, still feeling unsafe in my own space. But the police assured me 420delite was behind bars for good. With the help of trauma therapy, I slowly healed. I channeled my pain into advocacy, working to implement stronger protections for online creators. Six months later, I finally felt ready to dance freely once again. I started with small videos filmed right in my living room. Followers offered compassion as I rebuilt my platform. On the anniversary of my stalking ordeal, I posted a triumphant video dancing through the streets of my city. No longer confined - physically or emotionally. My soul was free. The trauma will always be part of me. But I refused to let it steal my spirit. As I danced boldly in the open sun, the only shadow was my own. I had reclaimed my light. My life. Myself.

CHAPTER 4

DEBBIE DOES DALLAS

LOOKING BACK NOW as a married English professor, it's chilling to recall my toxic romance in high school with the deeply unstable girl named Debbie. It was 1989 in Dallas Texas. Growing up there was nothing special about me. I was a naive teen; I mistook all the drama for passion. Debbie and I became infatuated fast with our junior year. It was your typically toxic high school romance at first, her extreme jealousy and possessiveness seemed almost flattering. I had no idea then how unhinged she truly was. It was my first serious relationship and I thought how I was being treated was normal. I thought all my friends' relationships were the same as I had with Debbie. The warning signs appeared early on in scribbled notes Debbie secretly slipped into my locker, veering from gushing affection to enraged accusations if I so much as glanced at another girl. Her mood swings gave me whiplash.

Debbie also started showing up unexpectedly to my basketball practices and church events, insisting we talk right that instant if I hadn't called her in a few hours. If I didn't comply, she'd create a scene, screaming at me at the top of her lungs until I gave in. And nothing is more humiliating in high school than people paying attention to you in a public space. I felt like I was emotionally being held hostage.

I soon felt like her prisoner, isolated from friends, and constantly walking on eggshells. But when I tried breaking things off, Debbie resorted to desperate measures - faking pregnancies and suicide attempts to reel me back in. I was too naive to realize she was manipulating me. I was always afraid that she might go off and hurt herself and it would be all my fault.

In senior year, Debbie's obsessive behavior escalated. She stole my class ring as proof I belonged to her. She also slashed the tires of a girl she thought I was interested in, though I barely knew her. I think I asked for a pencil in AP bio once but I can't even remember what her face looks like now. Terrified of what Debbie might do next, I finally found the courage to end it after discovering she'd been cheating on me with a close friend. Of course, Debbie denied everything and accused me of fabricating it out of jealousy. But even my friend had admitted to the encounter. At that point I saw my out and I was ready to take it. She had the nerve blame me for her cheating because I wasn't pay enough attention to her. Laughable right?

Now that I'd taken back control, Debbie ratcheted up her attempts to torment me. She flaunted her new relationship in my face, while still sending me unhinged letters declaring her undying love and vows to win me back. She'd even do something cheesy like writing down lyrics of love songs on my locket with her ever-classic white snake red lipstick. It was a bitch to clean off every time but there was no way to stop her. Debbie was just going to be Debbie. I kept my head down, counting the days until graduation and college freedom. At my graduation party, Debbie tried to humiliate me by showing up in a wedding dress, screaming we belonged together. I had to get a restraining order.

At college out-of-state, I slowly began to heal after cutting all contact with Debbie. In my senior year, I met my future wife, the opposite of Debbie. I tried putting that unhealthy chapter of my life behind me for good. If only it were that simple. After moving back home, I ran into Debbie at the grocery store. Her life had clearly unraveled since high school - divorced, lost a child. I pitied her, though remained guarded. Debbie still dumped heavy emotional baggage on me after mere minutes. But I wanted to avoid talking to her too much because the incident from the graduation still stuck with me. When she asked to meet for coffee, I declined, citing needing to check with my wife first. In truth, I had zero intention of seeing Debbie. The encounter left me unsettled.

I told my wife about running into my unstable ex. She found it odd Debbie overshared so intensely. I shrugged it off - that was just Debbie's way. As she would say it's a red flag, but I hadn't really thought about it and doubted I would run into her. The next day, a letter from Debbie awaited me at work. She apologized for cheating and mistreating me years ago. I wrote back thanking her, but suggested we cease contact for both our sakes. Clear right? I hoped that would be the end of it. But soon, more letters arrived from Debbie - each one more desperate and incoherent. She said she'd never stopped loving me and needed to see me again. I felt like lead had been pumped into my stomach. I remember thinking, oh god not again.

I tore the letters up, troubled by Debbie's escalating obsession. A few times, I thought I spotted her car parked outside my house at night. Had she found where I lived? How the heck did she find out where I lived? One letter contained a photo of me with my wife and kids at the park last weekend. How long had Debbie been following us? I began fearing for my family's safety.

The letters kept coming, nearly every day. Sometimes

my wife's face would be scratched out of the picture which gave me the chills. I honestly didn't know how far she would go. Then there were some days where the letters would contain violent threats against my wife unless I agreed to meet Debbie. Others professed limit-less devotion and promises to win me back. I started keeping the letters to start having a paper trail for this behavior. I informed campus security at my college about the situation. My home no longer felt like a haven with Debbie on the loose. I knew she was circling closer, but dreaded what unhinged act she might commit next. After repeated unanswered pleas for Debbie to stop contacting me, I finally went to the police station, clinging to the hope that they could make her deranged harassment cease.

Things had gotten out of hand. I brought the letters in as proof but the dismissive officers informed me that since Debbie hadn't physically assaulted anyone, their hands were tied. One even brazenly questioned if I had been secretly meeting up with Debbie behind my wife's back, implying I'd brought this nightmare upon myself. Is this what women went through when trying to get help? What if it was too late to get any legal help when she finally did snap. I left the precinct fuming, with no recourse to protect my family from Debbie's escalating madness. I'd naively thought the authorities would treat this as a serious threat. Now I felt utterly alone. A few days later, my wife came home from the store shaken and in tears. She told me Debbie had been lying in wait and accosted her in the parking lot. According to my wife, Debbie was disheveled, with dark circles under wildly darting eyes.

She had screeched at ear-splitting volume that my wife was a thief who had stolen away the life Debbie was meant to have with me. My wife had feared Debbie might physically attack her right then and there. My wife is not a confrontational woman in the least and this encounter shook her. I asked if Debbie had hurt her at all, and thankfully she hadn't laid a hand on her - this time. But seeing my wife so rattled and afraid enraged me. I knew then I had to come clean about Debbie's harassment campaign and the gravity of the threat she posed. Understandably upset I'd kept this disturbing situation from her, my wife still expressed relief to finally know the truth. At first, she too thought something too might have gotten on untoward as well. But when I explained the whole situation that is Debbie doing what Debbie does. We had a long embrace and concluded that our home was no longer safe from Debbie's intrusions. The very next evening, our worst fears were realized when our 12-year-old daughter let out a blood-curdling scream from her bedroom.

We rushed to find her pointing in horror at her closet

door, where I immediately spotted what had terrified her - a message scrawled in vivid red paint:

He will be mine!

The unhinged threat and the violation of Debbie having come into our little girl's room flooded me with fury and fear. I quickly installed new locks, security cameras, and a monitored alarm system. But these felt like feeble measures against Debbie's crazed obsession. It became painfully clear she would take more extreme steps to sabotage my family and reclaim what she irrationally viewed as hers. We no longer felt safe leaving our kids home unattended, not knowing what derangement Debbie might inflict on them. After taking indefinite leave from my teaching job to protect my family, I still felt powerless to stop her vile harassment. Debbie's methods were becoming more brazen and unpredictable. Seeing the unhinged glint in her eyes whenever she tracked me down, I knew Debbie would never cease her obsession on her own. Exhausted and desperate, I decided our only escape was to disappear entirely - change our names, relocate, go completely off the grid. It was the only way we'd ever be free of her torment.

But after months of quiet we finally felt safe enough to leave for a few hours for a date night. To be honest, it was needed. However, when we arrived home one night with my wife to a scene from my worst nightmares. Police swarmed our house, their patrol cars' red and blue lights flickering ominously in the darkness. My heart dropped as officers blocked us from going inside. Then came the words that made my blood run cold:

"Your ex-Debbie is in there holding your kids hostage."

Our courageous son Mark had dialed 911 and left the line open. The frantic dispatcher relayed that Debbie had tied up him and his sister, ranting crazily about taking them away to be her new children.

Rage and bone-chilling fear flooded through me. I strained against the officers holding me back, desperate to save my family from this madwoman. Inside, I could see shadows moving past the windows as a SWAT team took tactical positions around the house. I begged them to get my children out safely, imagining the terror they felt at Debbie's hands. After hours of failed negotiations, they suggested I talk to her using the megaphone, hoping my voice might lure her out. The thought of appealing to her warped obsession with me turned my stomach. But I would try anything to free my kids. I poured my heart out over the megaphone, telling her I still loved her, and we could run away together. The lies seared my tongue, but I continued pleading with the crazed stranger holding my children's lives in her hands.

Finally, the front door creaked open. I glimpsed Debbie's wild eyes darting around as she emerged, an eager smile stretching across her gaunt face.

"I knew you still loved me!", she cried out joyously before the police swarmed and restrained her. Her deranged screams of promises to reunite with me pierced the night as she disappeared into a squad car.

My children flew into my arms, pale and shaken but by some miracle unharmed. As Debbie was arrested, I met her lunatic gaze, this monster who had invaded the sanctity of my family's home. Everything had been ruined. We all collectively agreed that leaving town would be the best option.

We moved far away, uprooting my elderly mother in our desperate bid to escape the memories haunting that house. But Debbie's shadow followed us. My daughter woke up screaming from visions of her lurking. I still jump at every creak; certain Debbie was coming for what she viewed as hers. Her depraved delusions had nearly cost my children's lives. Peace would forever elude us after living through her twisted fantasy turned real. I constantly glanced over my shoulder, wondering if she would someday reappear to finish what she started.

CHAPTER 5

ANCHOR

AS A LOCAL TV REPORTER, I was thrilled when rumors circulated about me being considered for an anchor position. It would mean better hours and more time with my family. When I shared the news with my husband Dan, he seemed pleased but a bit reserved. Still, I was optimistic the flexible schedule and raise would smooth over any concerns. This was my shot to make a name for myself after years reporting live on the scene. Sure enough, my boss called me in with a smile and offered me the head anchor spot. I gladly accepted and almost floated back to my office, giddy with excitement for this new chapter ahead.

That night, Dan took me out to dinner to celebrate. But as I chatted happily about ideas for segments I could pitch now, he seemed distracted, just poking at his food, and giving one-word replies. I tried not to let his mood dampen mine. This was my time to shine. When the promotion was announced at the station, my co-workers were thrilled for me. Many said it was long overdue. I was touched by their sincere support, and energized to prove I deserved this opportunity. That first week on air flew by in a blur of scripts, teleprompters and familiarizing myself with the new role. It was daunting but exhilarating to introduce myself as lead anchor for the first time. I started getting recognized around town by enthusiastic viewers, which never got old.

Best of all were the fan letters that began pouring in. I'd receive dozens a day - sweet notes from kids asking how to be a reporter, thoughtful encouragement from older fans. I made a point to read them all and reply when I could. Dan gradually seemed to accept my new position and schedule, though he was often distracted and grew remote. I tried not to overanalyze it - this was just a big adjustment for us. One afternoon between broadcasts, I was sipping coffee and opening another batch of mail at my desk. I came across one letter with no return address, just my name in clipped-out magazine lettering. Figuring it was another viewer note, I opened it. But instead of praise, a single chilling sentence stared up at me in red letters:

"You're going to die, bitch."

I dropped the letter like it burned me, heart hammering in my chest.

I scanned the empty room as if the sender could be lurking in the shadows. Who would send something so twisted? Hands unsteady, I bagged the letter in a plastic sleeve and brought it to security. They said disturbing fan mail was unfortunately common for female broadcasters. They would investigate it but the letter provided few clues. I tried brushing it off but felt chilled to the bone. That night, I tossed and turned restlessly, the bloody text flashing behind my eyelids whenever I drifted off. At work I avoided opening fan mail, just giving it to assistants to screen first. But my anxiety grew when another letter arrived on plain stationary in machine-printed text:

"Enjoy your fame before it ends."

Each new message grew more specific and sinister, hinting at harm coming my way.

Security had no leads on who was sending them or how to make them stop. My mood shifted from unease to dread. I became jumpy walking to my car at night, feeling unseen eyes track my every move. Soft noises at home made me grab the nearest weapon in a panic. Dan grew impatient with my paranoia and fears, saying I was being irrational. He reminded me that hysteria caused by anonymous notes played right into the stalker's twisted goals. But even as I acknowledged the truth in his words, I couldn't shake the bone-chilling terror that this faceless monster was coming for me. That my growing fame had made me visible to some unknown darkness lurking closer each day. The threats preyed on my mind and pierced my once-optimistic outlook. Try as I might to power through with positivity, shadows encroached on the edges of my world. I knew the stalker fed off seeing me living in fear. But pretending nonchalance became impossible when I sensed malice around every corner. This poison pen pal had found the cracks in my armor, and fear was flooding in. The police kept urging me to go on with life as normal, advice which infuriated me - nothing about waiting helplessly for impending violence was "normal." But also, I knew they were right. I just prayed my resolve to thwart this terrorist would hold... For now, all I could do was plaster on a smile for the cameras and muddle through my broadcasts, hoping my fear didn't show through the mask. But as the empty threats and veiled menace continued unabated, I felt my grip on composure slipping day by perilous day.

After receiving the first chilling threat letter, I became obsessed with my work, staying late to distract myself from constantly looking over my shoulder. I asked my husband Dan to start picking me up at night and to install security cameras at our house. But he dismissed my fears as exaggerated. Frustrated by his apathy, I stopped asking for his help and leaned on my colleagues instead. They understood how serious the threats felt, even if the police didn't have much to act on yet. Soon the letters progressed to unsettling phone calls during my broadcasts. The caller would pose as a source or pretend to inquire about advertising rates. But then the voice would turn cruel and threatening, describing violent acts he planned to do to me. He clearly took sadistic pleasure in my stunned, speechless reactions before hanging up.

After each call, I had to regain composure and continue the broadcast, my hands shaking. I gave transcriptions of each sinister call to the police, begging them to trace the number. But the stalker always concealed his identity and changed disposable phones frequently. The calls were too short to track in real-time. The most the police could do was take reports, promising to step in if he escalated. Frustrated and fearful, I went to the head of the news station, ready to hand in my resignation for my own safety. But he revealed that they had already implemented call screening and established protocols to protect me in case of any threats. Knowing my employers took the stalker seriously helped me push through the constant harassment, even as it grew more frequent. I focused on my work, scoring high-profile interviews and exclusives.

One night, the station held an awards gala honoring the year's top reporters. To my shock, I won the coveted Anchor of the Year award, validation of my hard work under pressure. Dan accompanied me to the event and acted politely supportive.

But I sensed his subtle envy simmering beneath his smiles. We barely spoke as I glowed in my achievement. After the gala, we walked to our car in the parking garage, only to find all four tires viciously slashed. My award clattered to the ground as I cried out in alarm and outrage. Furious, Dan called the police while comforting me. I broke down in his arms, the vandalism feeling like the stalker's first physical trespass onto my world. Dan held me tightly, apologizing for not taking the threats seriously sooner. In the tense days that followed, Dan became my rock. He picked me up from work each night, scrutinized the viewer mail, and took my safety concerns seriously. I was moved by his attentiveness after months of minimization and arguments. But the stalker lay low after the tire incident, letting my panic reach fever pitch in the absence of direct contact. The police officially classified me as a high-risk target but had little else to offer except patrols by my home. I was on my own in this nightmare. Dan encouraged me to take a leave of absence for my mental health until the stalker was caught. But I refused to relinquish my career and passion to the terror this man cultivated in my psyche.

I would get through my broadcasts come hell or high water. Naively, I wondered if the tire slashing had fulfilled the stalker's sadistic urges for now. If his silence meant victory for me, or the quiet before an even darker storm. Though supported by colleagues, police and now Dan, I felt utterly alone in this fight against an unseen evil seemingly obsessed with destroying all I worked for. But giving up was not an option. I would stare down this monster and reclaim my life on my own terms. I only prayed that when the shattering climax came, I would have the strength left to survive it with my spirit intact.

For weeks after the tire slashing, the stalker lay low, leaving me anxious and on edge. One sleepless night, I went to the garage to sort old boxes and distract myself. Towards the back, I found a locked metal box. Curious, I tried different old combinations until it popped open on my own birthday. What I saw inside made my blood run cold. There were photos of me with my face violently scratched out, chilling letters in the stalker's handwriting, and the same red pen used to write the death threat note. Underneath was a burner phone with a voice changer attached. My heart dropped into my stomach. There was no denying the horrible truth - my stalker had been inside my own home all along. My doting, supportive husband, Dan was the one terrorizing me.

I slumped against the boxes, dizzy with shock and betrayal. My protector had meticulously orchestrated this campaign of terror against me. White-hot rage mingled with bone-deep fear. As quietly as possible, I put the incriminating contents back in the box and re-locked it. Confronting Dan outright could set him off. I had to get away safely first. Over the coming weeks, I secretly contacted divorce lawyers and TV networks out of state using my work computer. I lined up an anchor job two states away and made plans to rent a house there. When I told Dan about the "opportunity," he seemed pleased - if I rejected it. Confused, I insisted the kids, and I would only be gone a few years for my career. Dan grew reluctant to see me go, but the plans were already in motion. I promised to get housing and schools set up while he looked for work too. Anything to avoid raising his suspicions.

But we would never reunite there. On moving day, I had movers take the incriminating box to protect my evidence against Dan. He was oblivious. Once moved halfway across the country, I immediately filed for divorce and a restraining order, providing proof of Dan's stalking from the box. My fears were realized when the police had to swiftly intervene against Dan as his rage exploded. Confronted with the evidence I uncovered, Dan broke down and confessed everything in family court. He claimed neglect after my promotion drove him to terrorize me to get attention and control.

I stared numbly at this broken man I no longer recognized, feeling both hatred and pity before cutting all ties forever. He had no power over me now. The divorce was swift, and the court issued a permanent restraining order against Dan. I don't know where he disappeared to after that, and I never want to know. He is dead to me. But echoes of the trauma persist years later. I still look over my shoulder when alone outside at night. Unexpected calls make me freeze up momentarily. Triggers ambush me when least expected. I refuse to let lingering fear dominate my new identity and the life I've built far from that darkness though. I still work as a lead anchor and use my platform to advocate for victims of intimate partner abuse. Speaking my truth helps empower others and aids my own gradual healing. Nightmares come less frequently now. I gain strength seeing my resilience reflected in those I inspire. What happened will always haunt me on some level. But it does not define me. I stare down my fear and keep ascending to greater heights. My hard-won freedom is sweeter for the terrors I overcame to claim it. I am whole, I am worthy, I am brave - this is my mantra on difficult days. The shame is not mine to carry anymore. I am so much more than what was done to me then. And my light only grows brighter with time. I am finally free.

PUBLISHER'S EXCERPT

TALES OF TERROR: VOLUME 1

FOLLOWED BY EVIL

It's no secret that a lot of people like to retreat into the woods to escape the rigors of everyday life and reality in general. It's peaceful out there in the middle of mother nature and up until I was about fifteen years old, I felt the same way about it. However, once I had the experience I did while out camping with my best friend back in 1973, I have never been the same again. I also haven't ever gone into the woods again, for the most part, at night or even when it was dusk. Whatever we saw out there stayed with us and it's something that, though I've never physically seen it again, it has haunted my nightmares in all the years since. My best friend back then is still my best friend today and she and I share that evil experience and she feels the same way as I do about it. She also has nightmares and has avoided the woods at night at all costs ever since. No one believed us back then but for the most part, when we tell the story nowadays, people seem to at least give us the benefit of the doubt. We didn't do drugs or drink at all and in fact we weren't popular with most of the other kids in our school at the time because of our "goody goody" ways. That was neither here nor there for us and we enjoyed each other's company, as we still do. Here is the story of what happened to us and what could happen to you if you aren't careful and find yourself messing around with things you couldn't possibly understand.

Our families were friends as well so a lot of the time we would all vacation together. My best friend, Emily, had an older brother who was the same age as my own older brother, and she had one younger sister. Our mothers and fathers had all gone to high school together, the same high school we attended, in the same small town. We even had some of the same teachers as they did. I know that's wild when you really think about it, but it wasn't that uncommon back in those days. We grew up in rural Kentucky surrounded by roads that seemed to go on for miles and miles and lead to nowhere. Emily and I would spend hours walking along those roads and hanging out in the woods that surrounded them. There wouldn't be a house in sight, no signs of normal civilization and we could go hours without seeing or hearing another human being. She and I always had interests that other people considered bizarre and that our very religious parents were horrified by. We thought it was all in good fun, as we learned new ways to try and divine our futures and connect with the spirit world. We knew our parents had an end of the school year camping trip planned for all of us and we decided it was a good idea to sneak a Ouija board in with our stuff. The way we ended up with that board is another story altogether, but it isn't too relevant to the encounter we ended up having so I will just say we stole it from a shop near our home. The owner of the shop was said to be a devil worshiper and a witch, but not a good one. She was a mean old woman who seemed to hate kids our age and getting it out of the store was a mission in and of itself. However, I often wonder now if the old hag knew all along what we were doing and what we had done, and if it was her doing, what happened to us.

We all set off in a campervan, but we weren't going to all be staying in it together. It was big enough for the twelve-hour drive and seven people, but it wouldn't sleep all of us. Me and Emily and both of our brothers would sleep outside with our parents and her baby sister inside. It was the first year the adults would be sleeping inside and allowing us kids to sleep on the outside and we were excited. Our older brothers were typical for that time, and they mocked and picked on us relentlessly so she and I had a plan that we thought would work and allow us the time, space, and privacy we needed to use the pilfered board. Eventually we got to the campsite and spent the whole night hanging out by the fire, eating, and having a great time with our families. Eventually though it was time to go to sleep and that's when Emily and I enacted our plan. We picked a fight with our brothers and then begged our parents to let us go further into the woods, just a little bit, so we could have some privacy overnight. They eventually relented because they knew our brothers would be right there within ear shot. Also, they knew no matter how much we fought they wouldn't let anything happen to us should they hear us screaming or otherwise in some distress. I could tell our moms were nervous, but they let us go and Emily and I walked for about five minutes deeper into the woods. We only needed it to be far enough away that the boys wouldn't hear our whispers or notice the tealight candles we planned on lighting during our Ouija board session.

Emily and I had some whispered conversations about how to use the board. We had recently watched a horror movie that had a Ouija board in it, and everyone died at the end except one person. You would think that would have deterred us from ever even going near one, but you would be wrong, and it only made us want to try one even more. Back in the early seventies, where we come from, it was considered evil and demonic to want to speak with the dead, but Emily and I were just planning on asking it basic and somewhat silly questions about boys we liked and teachers we didn't like, stuff like that. We weren't taking it seriously at all and that was our first, worst and biggest mistake. As soon as we no longer heard our brothers, we took the board and the candles out. We were both sitting on our sleeping bags across from one another and we had the board in the middle. The only candles we had were four little, half used tea lights that we had taken from my mother's office. We lit the candles, and the air was still so they weren't immediately going out or anything. One strange thing we did notice is that as soon as our fingers hit the planchette, the forest seemed to go very quiet, and very still, suddenly. It freaked us out a little bit but again, it wasn't something that we were going to allow to deter us. We were frightened but excited and we giggled the whole time. At first, we asked if anyone was there, and the planchette immediately moved to the word "goodbye." That happened three times, but we didn't take the hint and continued trying to get something to communicate with us. We asked for the fourth time if anyone was there and the planchette moved to "yes." I knew Emily wasn't moving it and she knew that I wasn't, and we both immediately took our hands off the board. We were scared and both of us had a bad feeling. Still though, we pressed on. After a few minutes of establishing a connection, a spirit came through that claimed to be my grandfather. He had recently passed, and it had been very hard on me. He and I were super close and losing him had devastated me. I was in tears as I asked questions that only he would know the answers to and every single time the board, which I thought my grandfather was communicating with me through from beyond the grave, knew all the right answers.

This went on for about five minutes, the exchange with my "grandfather." Suddenly things started to get very scary. A very strong gust of wind came out of nowhere in the otherwise calm and windless night. It didn't only blow the candles out completely, but it sent two of them flying into the woods like they were made of feathers instead of hard wax and a metal base. At the same time, the planchette flew off the board and hit a nearby tree. We heard growling coming from some-where in the woods, very close to us, right when the wind stopped blowing and the candles and planchette had landed. We didn't scream because honestly at that point we were more scared of our families catching us than we were of what we thought could have just been a little series of strange coincidences. We were both shaking and once the growling stopped, I started to giggle. I giggled and laughed a lot when I was very nervous and didn't know what else to do. Emily was giggling too, but I think she was doing it more to try and calm herself down. We decided to collect the candles and the planchette and hide the board in the woods. We knew we were supposed to get it to say "goodbye" before stopping the session with it, but we were inexperienced and decided to just ditch the board in the woods and get rid of the candles. I got up to collect the candles and told Emily to collect the board and planchette. She was reluctant and instead said she would keep watch to make sure no one from our fami-lies was coming close to us so that we didn't get caught. I hadn't thought of that and so I agreed to just collect everything and put it all into my bag. We were going to walk further into the woods, just a little bit, and hide everything. When we left to go home, we would just leave it there. Whatever we conjured that night, which wasn't my dearly departed grandfather, had other plans for us though.

I told Emily to keep watch while I walked and hid everything. She agreed and was happy not to have to go further into the woods or even touch that board again. We were both filled with terror and instant regret about what we had done. We would make sure we prayed later to find forgiveness because we also felt very guilty for using the spirit board. That's what we called it back then by the way, a spirit board. I felt like I was being followed the entire time I was looking with my flashlight for a place to put the board and candles where we wouldn't accidentally come across it when walking around with our parents and siblings. I heard a growling sound and when I turned to look there were two sets of red eyes peering at me from behind the trees. I screamed and dropped everything right there where I stood. I ran back to tell Emily what had happened. I felt like something was running behind me the entire way and I could hear the growling right next to my ear as though whatever it was, it was almost right on top of me. Emily and I took a long time to calm down and we tried to pray but kept being scared by the growling and losing our concentration. We looked around and all we saw were the two sets of red eyes looking at us, but we didn't see what was attached to them at first. Eventually, I think from adrenaline alone, we both passed out. I woke up to Emily screaming and when I looked over at her she was being dragged around in her sleeping bag. I will never forget the look of terror in her eyes and on her face at that moment. I looked up and suddenly there was a gigantic shadow figure hovering over me as I laid there, helpless to help either myself or my friend. I tried to scream but nothing would come out. The entity had red eyes that exuded evil and malicious intent. It smelled like someone was burning their trash nearby, but I knew it was the entity itself. It had a hood over its head. Eventually a small shriek escaped my throat, and I was able to move again. I jumped up and ran over to my best friend and asked if she was okay. She said that she was but we both had scratches all over our legs and arms. She had tears in her sleeping bag as if a grizzly bear had swiped it or something. We didn't know what to do and were shocked when no one came running at the sounds of our screaming.

We put her sleeping bag back across from mine and just sat there, crying, and trying to comfort one another. Our scratches were bleeding a little bit, and later we saw they were only scrapes. As we sat there, we heard growling and the wind picked up again. Whatever was out there wasn't done with us yet. Two shadow beings, both about twelve or thirteen feet tall with red eyes and a shadowy hood walked out of the wilderness beyond where we were sitting. The hoods dropped from their heads and what we saw were the most grotesque and hideous beings or creatures we had ever seen. Their skin seemed like it was burning off their faces. They had green fangs for teeth and huge, puss filled globs all over their faces. They were slowly floating towards us, and it was almost like we were in one of the terrifying but very cheesy horror movies we loved to watch so much. It didn't take either one of us any consideration and we got up and ran to the campervan to tell our parents what had happened. In typical style of religious parents, they were only focused on the fact we had used the board and not anything else that we had been through. We got in so much trouble and once we were back home, we were both grounded for the entire summer. We also under-went something like an exorcism at church and honestly, I think that's what saved us from being haunted, hunted and overtaken by those two demons from hell that either dwelt in those woods already or who we summoned from the board. Maybe it was a little bit of both.

————

TALES OF TERROR: VOLUME 1

CHAPTER 6

CLOWNING AROUND

I'D BEEN LOOKING FORWARD to tonight for weeks. Our state capital puts on an amazing Halloween festival at the fairgrounds every year, and all my friends were finally going together. I couldn't wait to hit all the haunts and mazes. After waiting in the long line, we made our way through the front gates as darkness fell. Fog swirled around the grounds and creepy music filled the air. It was a perfect spooky ambience. My friends and I wore matching *final girl* costumes. I always identified with those resilient heroines who outsmart the killer in horror movies. As we took cheesy posing photos, I noticed a creepy clown off to the side with his face painted like the alien clowns from *Killer Klowns from Outer Space* - one of my favorite horror flicks. I had to take a pic with him. "Hey, love the costume!" I called out.

The clown turned and, in a gravelly voice, thanked

me. Up close, the makeup was incredibly detailed. As we posed together, he said, "You look beautiful tonight, like the final girl who makes it to the end."

I laughed nervously, unsure if he was staying in character or complimenting me. Still, I thanked him for humoring me and rejoined my friends. We hit the carnival rides first, screaming our heads off on the rollercoasters and bumper cars. As we waited in line for the log flume, I could have sworn I saw that creepy clown standing in the shadows at the ride's entrance, watching me. But when I looked again, he was gone. I shrugged it off, though a small shiver went through me. Once we dried off from the flume's plunge, we headed for the event's famous haunted maze.

My friends dared me to go first into the thick fog that concealed the maze's entrance. Sweeping the fog aside like a curtain, I tentatively made my way forward. The fog muffled all light and sound, leaving me in eerie isolation. But eventually a doorway emerged, and I entered the dark maze. Terrifying figures jumped out at every turn as I navigated the labyrinth alone. My heart raced, but I laughed in exhilaration. I loved the adrenaline rush of being scared in a safe, controlled way. The maze eventually emptied out into an indoor haunted house. Loud shrieks and chainsaw sounds assaulted me as I carefully walked through displays of gruesome scenes. At one point, I thought I glimpsed the creepy clown from earlier blended in with a tableau of other monsters. But he was gone in a blink. At last, I escaped out the back. My friends waited outside, screaming as I burst out.

We shared our scare stories, then headed to the final attraction - a disorienting house of mirrors. As we wound through the mirrored corridors, struggling to find the exits, our reflections jumped out at us every-where. My friends dared me to close my eyes and navi-gate blindly to the next room. I took the challenge. Alone in the dark and surrounded by mirrors, I became easily confused. Just as I considered giving up, I opened my eyes. For a split second in the glass, I saw the freaky clown right behind me before he darted out of sight. I yelped in alarm, stumbling away. Suddenly a hand grabbed my arm and I nearly screamed before realizing it was just my friend, who had come back to find me. Catching my breath, I tried explaining what I'd seen.

My friends just laughed, guessing I'd imagined things after being in the dark too long. But I couldn't shake the twisting nervousness in my gut. Something about that clown lurking around all night felt wrong. We took a food break, sipping hot cider and people watching. As we sat eating, I noticed the clown standing under a distant streetlamp, illuminated in the shadows. He waved slowly at me with a twisted grin when he saw me staring. I pointed him out to my friends, feeling vali-dated, but they just rolled their eyes.

"The actors are supposed to scare people, it's their job," one said. "They probably get bonuses for freaking out girls like you."

My unease grew. We hit a few more rides before stopping by a psychedelic exhibition with swirling lights and trippy music. As we entered the visualization tunnel clogged with fog, I was distracted by the dizzying experience. About halfway through, I glanced behind us and saw the clown had followed us inside. He stood motionless, tracking me with his gaze and smiling malevolently. Then the strobes shifted and he vanished. I urgently told my friends I wanted to leave.

They tried reassuring me it was just part of the show. But I insisted we go, unable to voice my inexplicable dread. As we exited, I looked back once more. The clown stood inside the still-foggy tunnel, watching me depart. My friends said I was letting my imagination run wild, but I couldn't shake the sinister feeling. We left the fairgrounds soon after, the playful mood of the night having shifted into something ominous. I saw no more of the clown on our way out.

After the unnerving encounter with the creepy clown, my friends and I decided to take a food break to calm down. The fair had awesome themed food carts, like "brain tacos" and "blood sausage sandwiches." Perfect fuel for an evening of frights. We sat at a picnic table laughing at the gory eats, but I couldn't fully relax. That smiling clown face lurked in my mind, dampening the mood. As we ate, prickles of unease ran across my skin. I scanned the crowds, unable to shake the sense of unseen eyes tracking me. My friends noticed my discomfort and assured me I was letting the atmosphere get to me.

"You're totally getting your money's worth for scares," they teased.

I tried to play along, but the twisting nervousness persisted. After eating, we debated where to head next and settled on another haunted mansion.

As we approached the entrance, I began having second thoughts. Something about the looming facade filled me with inexplicable dread. But I let my friends convince me inside. We slowly worked our way through the elaborate haunted house displays. Creepy portraits with eyes that followed guests, furniture that rocked back and forth on its own, disembodied voices whispering in the darkness. Textbook creep show stuff, but eerily effective. Deeper inside, we reached a room with arms sticking out of the walls lined with holes. As people squeezed through, the hands would reach out and brush against them lightly. I tensed, already unnerved. Halfway through the room, I felt a hand close tightly around my ankle. I looked down with a shriek to see the unmistakable white glove of a clown. My stomach dropped. As I shook the hand off in panic, my friends froze, wide-eyed.

"They're not supposed to grab people..." one said slowly.

I backed out of the room, heart racing. Had I imagined the clown hand? But my friends' stunned faces suggested otherwise. We hurried outside, where I tried calming my shaking nerves. "I must be overtired and on edge," I reasoned aloud, hoping for reassurance.

My friends hesitantly agreed that was likely the case. We laughed weakly and decided to head for one final attraction to end the night. The massive, haunted barn loomed at the edge of the fairgrounds, and townspeople raved about it annually. As we approached, a bloodcurdling scream rang out from inside that stopped me in my tracks. My friends tugged me along, amped for one last adrenaline rush. Reluctantly, I followed them in, eyes darting around nervously as we waited in line. A facade of a decrepit old barn surrounded us, embellished with disturbing props. Something about the way the walls seemed to completely enclose us left me deeply unsettled. At last, an employee ushered us through a side door into the maze of horrors within. We crept through the dark, gore-filled scenes, clinging to each other and screaming. Despite my frazzled state, I had to admit the sets were impressive. Then, as we turned a corner, I glimpsed something that turned my blood to ice.

The clown stood at the end of the corridor, under a flickering light. I only caught its twisted face for a split second before it retreated into darkness. I grabbed my friend's arm with a gasp. She gave me a worried look, reminding me nicely that it wasn't real, just a scary tactic. But my gut twisted sharply. I quickened our pace, hair rising on my neck. The final stretch inside was a disorienting labyrinth of rooms and noise effects that left me shrinking into my group in fear. My senses straining, I no longer felt immersed in a thrilling haunted house. I felt hunted. At last, we stumbled out the back exit, escaping into the cool night air. As I gulped lungful's of air, my friends tried lifts my spirits with jokes about finding me some chill pills.

But I was long past laughter. I couldn't articulate why, but every instinct screamed we needed to get far away from this place, now. As we headed to the exit, I resisted the urge to break into a panicked run. I didn't look back at those looming barns, certain a pair of grinning eyes watched me flee into the darkness beyond the safety of the bright fairgrounds. My friends' voices sounded distant and tinny as we left the festival behind. I felt in my bones that the night was far from over. Whether real or imagined, something had marked me tonight. The cold October wind bit through me, foretelling icy days ahead. I could hardly wait to barricade myself in the security of home. But an insidious voice in my mind whispered that soon nowhere would be safe...

As we entered the final haunted attraction, a claustrophobic fog enveloped us, separating me from my friends. Alone and blinded, my heart pounded wildly. I called out but heard only eerie silence. The fog muffled all light and sound. I slowly felt my way through, flinching as disturbing shapes emerged then vanished in the gloom. Turn after turn, I found no exit from the oppressive fog. Panic rising, I strained my ears for any sign of my friends, to no avail. Just when I thought I couldn't take it anymore, the fog cleared ahead. Relieved, I emerged into an elaborate haunted house set. But my momentary comfort dropped when I glimpsed a familiar face leering at me from the shadows. The creepy clown stood at the end of the hall, illuminated in a flickering light. Our eyes locked, and he broke into an unnatural grin, slowly approaching me.

I backed away, terrified. Despite my friends' reassurances, I knew this was no ordinary performer. His twisted delight at my fear confirmed my worst fears - I was being stalked, toyed with. Hunted. I turned and ran desperately through the haunted house, barging blindly through hidden doors and cobwebbed corridors. Bombastic noise effects made me scream and cower, but I couldn't stop. Everywhere I turned, more ghoulish figures jumped out. But they were just props and actors. The real monster pursued me through the twisting maze, always one room behind yet never letting me escape his sights. At last, I burst out of a door into a hall of mirrors.

Infinite reflections of myself flashed in every direction, but none of my friends were visible. I was alone. Or so I thought - until creeping up behind me in the glass crawled the image of the clown, his smile now a grotesque rictus grin. He reached towards me with gloved hands. I released a raw, primal scream. Without thinking, I tore down the mirrored corridor, the clown drawing closer in the glass with each step. I saw an exit ahead.

Almost there... Suddenly, a reflection of my friend appeared ahead, calling my name. In desperation I veered towards it - straight into solid glass. Pain exploded in my head and hot blood gushed down my face. Dazed, I collapsed to the floor. The clown seized the opportunity and lunged, pinning me down. I sobbed and struggled as his gloves grasped at my clothes. Through the red haze I saw his mixture of manic glee and cold rage up close, more terrifying than any mask. Summoning my last burst of strength, I screamed and thrashed, buying precious seconds. Suddenly, the pressure released as approaching footsteps echoed down the hall. He was fleeing before being caught. My friends burst in, freezing at the sight of my blood-drenched self-writhing on the floor.

They helped me up and out of that house of horrors, shooting panicked looks behind us as we fled. Outside, the cool night air revived me, though my head was spinning, and foreign blood coated my face, blinding me. Screams rang out as we emerged, drawing worried crowds. The guards rushed over, demanding to know what happened. As they examined my injury, I haltingly told them about the clown stalking us all night, attacking me in the maze. The guards exchanged ominous looks and began combing the haunted houses for him. Medics bandaged my aching head as my friends recounted their stories, equally shaken. Their dismissal of my fears now seemed a grave mistake as the reality sunk in. We had been preyed upon all evening. And I bore the physical and mental scars to prove it. Guilt mixed with lingering fear on their faces. They held me as I trembled uncontrollably, the image of that clown's lunging hands etched forever behind my eyes.

We all agreed to give our statements to the police soon. As the crowds gawked, I suddenly wished desperately to be anywhere but here. Then across the sea of faces I made direct eye contact with a still figure - a man in black, ordinary looking. Before I could process why, he gave me a sly little wave...and vanished. My heart seized. Had he been a conspirator? Or was I now imagining threats everywhere I looked? The head wound was clearly distorting my perception as the night's terror left me grasping for phantoms. Nonetheless, I refused to stay on those fairgrounds another minute. The police tried convincing us to walk them through the attractions where I'd been assaulted, to identify my attacker. But the thought of seeing that clown's grinning facade emerge from the darkness again paralyzed me.

My friends managed to talk the cops into letting us give official statements tomorrow, once we'd recovered somewhat. I knew my psyche would never fully recover from this violation of safety and trust. But for now, I needed to go home. My friends drove me, as I sobbed convulsively in shock. Soon I was huddled under blankets in bed, lights blazing, reduced to a shaken child in an adult's battered body. Visions of leering clown faces flashed whenever I closed my swollen eyes. I knew the long process of healing from this trauma would forever change me. I used to love immersing myself in artificial fear, trusting those spaces to be safe outlets for darkness. But that illusion had been forever shattered tonight. Because sometimes, true evil disguises itself in the same shadows that fascinate us most. And once you have stared into its vacant eyes, once its hands have seized you against your will...the lights never fully return. A small, broken part of you remains trapped in that darkness, warning you to never drop your guard again. Your trust in those shadows extinguished forever.

CHAPTER 7

CRUNCHY ROLL

AS A STRUGGLING 20-something in New York City, working two exhausting jobs was my reality for years. Ordering late night takeout became a guilty pleasure I could conveniently afford. My favorite was a little hole-in-the-wall sushi spot called Little Hong's. Their spicy tuna rolls were to die for, and they stayed open until 4am, perfect for my hectic schedule. The son of the owner, Jeff, often delivered my orders no matter how late I called them in. He was only a few years older than me - quiet but friendly. I appreciated how hard he and his family worked.

Jeff soon memorized my usual order - crunchy tempura shrimp rolls with extra spicy mayo on the side. Whenever he arrived with my food, he'd give me a polite smile and wish me a good night before heading back down to the shop. After slogging away during my daily grind, those savory late-night meals were small but much needed bright spots. The reliability of Jeff's deliveries was comforting in a city where I felt so alone. But after years of burning the candle at both ends, I finally landed a 9 to 5 office job at a law firm. I finally had the means to cook more instead of ordering takeout and kept much earlier hours. It was nice to be able to take care of myself once again.

No longer needing Little Hong's delivery services regularly, I ordered from them only occasionally for old times' sake. Even then, Jeff's father would bring the food since it was during the day. I missed chatting with Jeff on those late nights when it felt like just the two of us in the sleeping city. But my sanity and wallet appreciated the extra time and savings. One morning I awoke to find a familiar bag sitting outside my apartment door - my favorite tempura shrimp roll order from Little Hong's. Puzzled, I checked the receipt. This had been delivered around 3am. Obviously I couldn't eat sushi that had sat out overnight. But I made a mental note to drop by the restaurant later to thank them for the thoughtful surprise gesture.

Work kept me busy and I forgot to stop in that day. But the next morning, yet another order from Little Hong's waited on my doorstep - now with a post-it note attached. In neat handwriting it read:

Bon appétit! Enjoy your day!

Perplexed but touched they kept sending my usual order, I resolved to visit first thing after work. That afternoon, I headed to Little Hong's to thank them for the mystery deliveries. But when I told Mr. Hong the story, a troubled look crossed his face.

"My son hasn't done late night deliveries in months," he said slowly. "Especially not to your neighborhood."

My stomach dropped as I glanced at Jeff busing tables nearby.

After the unsettling discovery that Jeff had been delivering food to my home unasked, I decided going out more with coworkers might help me feel safer. We often met for happy hours at bars near the office. But one night, I froze in dismay to see Jeff waiting by the entrance, takeout bag in hand. He must have followed me from work somehow. He tried repeatedly to bring me drinks from the bar. I politely declined each time, deeply unsettled. How had he even known I'd be here tonight?

I cut the evening short, thoroughly rattled. It was clear Jeff was showing up places deliberately to seek me out. I decided to steer clear of going out anywhere for a while. The next morning, a bouquet of flowers waited on my doorstep. Attached was a note with Jeff's phone number, asking why I wouldn't talk to him. Filled with frustration, I called and stated bluntly that I wasn't interested in any relationship. I asked him to cease contact. After hanging up, I felt hopeful I'd made my stance clear. But I awoke the following day to another floral delivery - this time rotted and crawling with maggots.

My blood turned to ice reading the note attached:

"I hope you rot just as quickly."

Hands shaking, I threw the vile bouquet away. Then I called Little Hong's, begging them to stop their son from harassing me. Mr. Hong was shocked to hear about Jeff's behavior. Apparently, he'd claimed we were practically engaged. I adamantly denied any romantic ties. They promised to speak with Jeff and ensure he stayed away. Relief swept over me. Finally, this nightmare would end. Weeks passed without incident. One evening, I felt at ease enough to walk home alone from the train as dusk fell over the city.

Suddenly, footsteps rapidly approached behind me on the sidewalk. Before I could react, Jeff appeared and struck me hard across the face. An explosion of pain shot through me as I collapsed on the pavement. I saw a deranged look in his eyes as he towered over me, hand raised to strike again. Mercifully, I blacked out after the next blows landed. I drifted in and out of consciousness, only vaguely aware of a neighbor finding me. I remember reaching out and mumbling something, but the entire thing is a blur. Why did Jeff do this? I had only turned him down for a date. I had never been cruel or mean to him or turned down these gifts with distaste, there was no way I had deserved such a thing and I think that is what helped me to get through.

When I came to three days later in the hospital, a dull throbbing enveloped my face. The doctor said I was lucky to be alive after the vicious attack. I recounted the full stalking nightmare to the police from my hospital bed. They promptly arrested Jeff. But the ensuing trial was a bigger nightmare. Jeff maintained our "love" and his innocence. I had to painfully recount all the harassment I'd endured leading up to his brutal ambush. I'd never felt so cold and so hot at the same time. I drifted somewhere in the back of my eyes and I was so cold.

In the end, he was found guilty on all counts. But the experience left me a shaken shell. I put in for an immediate transfer at work, needing to flee the city where I no longer felt safe. My physical recovery in the hospital was long and painful. The blows I sustained left the entire right side of my face shattered - fracture lines spider-webbed across my cheekbone, eye socket, and jaw.

The pain was excruciating, despite heavy pain medication. Any movement of my head sent stabbing sensations through my face. The doctors worried my right eye might have permanent damage from the beating. For the first week, my face was too swollen and bruised for doctors to fully assess the injuries. I could barely open my right eye to a slit. I struggled to eat or speak normally with my wired jaw.

When the swelling finally decreased, the full extent of damage became clear. My cheekbone would require reconstructive surgery with metal plates. And my right eye remained bloodshot and blurry, the orbital bone surrounding it having been broken in several places. After a second grueling surgery to repair my crushed orbital socket, I faced months of vision therapy to strengthen my eye which had sustained nerve damage. Double vision blurred peripheral vision, and loss of depth perception became my new normal.

I attended weekly physical therapy to rebuild strength and mobility in my stiff, aching jaw. The constant clicking and throbbing made even simple tasks like chewing agonizing. Worst was the phantom pain - my brain continued misfiring signals of pain long after the wounds had closed. I often awoke convinced Jeff was in the act of smashing my face again. The psychological recovery was equally challenging. I started panicking anytime I needed to walk outside after dusk. I saw Jeff's face in crowds, always fearing he would reappear.

Loud voices and people approaching unexpectedly from behind triggered panic attacks, sending me back to that sidewalk where my life nearly ended at his hands.

Though Jeff was locked away, he still haunted my thoughts and physical being. His deranged act of violence left scars far deeper than the ones marring my face. These days, I can't walk alone at night without seeing Jeff's shadowy figure approaching. I'll never touch a crunchy shrimp roll again that will remind me of the innocence before this madness.

Jeff may be locked away, but he still haunts my thoughts. The broken face in the mirror serves as a constant reminder that evil can disguise itself as kindness before revealing its true nature. You can never really tell what is going through one's mind. It could be as simple as something good or something of a more intense nature. It wasn't until I had a brick bashed upside the head. It wasn't fair, it wasn't asked for despite what some people had the nerve to say to. No one deserves that kind of treatment.

CHAPTER 8
SLEEPING BEAUTY

AS A BROKE COLLEGE STUDENT, I was thrilled when I saw a flyer looking for participants in a sleep study. The pharmaceutical company was testing a new medication and needed volunteers to trial it under observation for a few nights a week. The money they offered was too good to pass up. All I had to do was take a pill before bed and sleep at their research facility three times a week while they monitored my vitals and rest patterns. Easy enough for some quick cash. I was one of 10 participants starting the trial together. We were briefed on potential side effects of the experimental sleep aid, but they seemed mild.

A doctor explained they needed to keep us multiple nights to evaluate the effects over time. The first couple nights at the facility, I slept surprisingly great. The medication knocked me out quickly and I woke up feeling refreshed. Aside from some grogginess wearing off, I felt fine. But halfway through the first week, I began waking up with mild muscle soreness. Figuring it was just a side effect of the new medication, I reported it during my daily health checks. The doctors made note of it but didn't seem concerned. Soon the muscle pain worsened and spread. My calves and thighs ached constantly, making it hard to walk far.

The pain kept me tossing and turning all night, interfering with sleep. I reported the escalating symptoms and asked to stop taking the pills. But the doctors said quitting midway would compromise the whole study. The pain was tolerable, so they advised me to push through the week and they would adjust the dosage. I figured it would wear off the long I took the medication. Reluctantly, I continued, even as the cramps and spasms worsened by the day. Their doctors did a physical and everything came back ok.

Though alarmed by the bizarre symptoms, they cleared me to complete the trial. Only a few nights left and I'd get paid. So, I suffered through the agony when I was at the clinics but and slept little. On the final day, could barely get out of bed. It felt like my whole body had clenched up overnight. I shuffled stiffly through the exit exams before demanding to go home. In the weeks following, I expected the pain to fade since I stopped the pills. But if anything, it grew more severe and spread to my core abdominal muscles. My appointments with doctors and specialists were deeply puzzling to them. All my test results came back normal.

No vitamin deficiencies, autoimmune issues, spinal injuries. No medical explanation for the inexorable tightening of my body. Simple tasks like dressing or bathing were enormous feats due to the cramping. Sleep never brought relief, only semi-consciousness. Desperate, I asked the pharmaceutical company if any other trial participants reported similar ongoing issues. But they claimed the medication had no lasting effects once discontinued. No answers and no end in sight, I sank into hopeless despair. This trial was supposed to be an easy paycheck, not the catalyst of my bodily downfall. All I could do was research experimental treatments and wait for the next wave of seizing agony, terrified of what would shutter closed next. Somehow, I knew this wrenching descent was only beginning. The medication seemed to have unlocked something latent inside me, subtly reshaping my flesh against its - and my - will. Where it would end was a nightmare I dared not imagine. But one I lived nonetheless, trapped in my own stiffening skin.

Weeks into the trial, my painful muscle spasms and stiffness persisted. Puzzled, my doctor sent me for all kinds of tests - MRIs, CT scans, bloodwork. But nothing abnormal showed up. Frustrated, my doctor asked me to come in for a full physical just to rule things out. As I lay on the exam table, she felt my stiff limbs and joints, frowning. But since it was time for my yearly exam we moved on from the pain and focused on my feminine health portion of my physical.

She did a Pap smear, collecting samples to check for any abnormalities. I stared at the speckled ceiling, praying she could find some explanation for my suffering. The doctor told me to get dressed and wait in her office to discuss the results. When I sat down across from her, the doctor's face was somber. She said the Pap smear showed atypical cell changes indicating possible cervical damage. I sat there numb, unable to comprehend her words. Slowly, she asked if I had been sexually active recently or noticed any abnormal bleeding. I shook my head, confused. I was too busy with school and the study to date anyone. It had honestly been months since I had been with anyone.

The doctor's voice remained professional but gentle as she said the cell changes were consistent with injuries from assault. My mind reeled - there was no way, I would know...wouldn't I? Seeing my shock, she asked if I would consent to a rape kit to gather more evidence. I couldn't form words, just nodding as the ground crumbled beneath my world. Everything after that was fog. A kind nurse came in and began meticulously swabbing, photographing, and collecting samples from my entire body. I sat there violated, disconnected from reality. As they sealed up the rape kit, the doctor squeezed my shoulder, promising they would get to the bottom of this.

I somehow stumbled out to my car in a haze. The world felt off-kilter, shadows around me skewed dark and menacing. What had been done to my unconscious form without my knowledge or consent? The very question shattered my sense of safety. Dread filled me thinking back to my overnight stays at the research facility. They had round-the-clock video monitoring of our rooms, right? It would show if anyone came in at night. I confronted the pharmaceutical company with the evidence of assault, demanding they review the footage. But they insisted no staff had entered my room outside of scheduled observations. No footage supported my claims.

When the police investigated with a warrant, the company indignantly provided the files. Again, they showed undisturbed sleep each night, despite the stark physical evidence. It made no sense. The doctor said the injuries were not self-inflicted. And no one else had access to me during that time. How could this be? The more I searched for answers, the more dead ends I hit. Even the rape kit bore no useful traces - no strands of hair or identifiable fluids present to analyze for DNA. It was like a ghost had violated my comatose body night after night. But the worsening pain testified otherwise.

Something real had entered my room, my body, and left twisted evidence of its trespass inside me. I could no longer write it off as a side effect of medication. I withdrew from my remaining classes, wracked by horrific images of faceless violators I couldn't recall. The police investigation stalled with no leads.

My own mother even gently asked if I was just looking for attention or a payout. But no authorities believed me. They shook their heads, citing the tapes showing undisturbed sleep. Post-traumatic stress, they reasoned. Some fugue state mental break. It was easier to label me crazy than accept the impossible truth. But I had the medical evidence etched into my cells, the pain that clamped down tighter every day. And no one could take those very real pieces of the puzzle from me. I knew I wasn't insane. Something was stolen from me in the night. But by what force, earthly or otherwise, I was no closer to understanding. Time was running out to prove my sanity and solve the invoking riddle of my body's distress. But each chilling dead end only seemed to rule out all-natural explanation. And as the merciless cramping ensnared me, I feared that whatever entered me under the cloak of night had truly claimed my physical form. Until I reclaimed my memory and found answers, this evil owned me more completely than I could possibly grasp.

Weeks after the inconclusive investigation, police

reached out asking if I'd assist in a sting operation to catch my assaulter. They now believed multiple women had been abused during overnight pharmaceutical trials. The lead detective explained they narrowed it down to three male staffers with nighttime access to patients' rooms. If I went back for one more study night, they were confident they could lure out and catch the perpetrator. Though utterly terrified to return there, I agreed. I needed closure and justice, not just for me but all the shadowy victims who were violated under the guise of "research." When the night came, my heart rattled in my chest as I entered the too-familiar facility and got set up in a room rigged with hidden cameras.

I pocketed my dose of pills, planning to stay awake all night. The lights went out at midnight, and I lay stiffly in the bed, every muscle taut. The detective assured me they were right outside monitoring everything. But alone in the dark, my fear was primal. At exactly 3am, the door slowly creaked open. I clenched my fists, breath frozen in my lungs. Quiet footsteps crept closer and I felt a dip in the mattress. Steeling myself, I covertly grabbed my phone and dialed the detective's number as the figure slid under my sheets. As his hands roamed my rigid body, I coiled every fiber of my being to keep still, suppressing shuddering revulsion. Just as the assaulter reached for my clothes, the lights blazed on and police swarmed the room.

"Freeze! Hands in the air!" they yelled, tackling him off the bed.

I scrambled back against the wall, shaking and fighting nausea as they cuffed the orderly from the night shifts. The towering man who had haunted my nightmares for weeks.

One officer came over and gently wrapped a jacket around my shoulders as I dissolved into heaving sobs. It was over. My monster had a face and a name now. And soon, a prison sentence. In the weeks that followed, the full extent of the orderly's violations emerged. He had taken trophies - stolen clothing, vials of blood, even snippets of hair from his unconscious victims. Police also uncovered how he followed several women home, attempting to break in and continue his assaults. He had staked out my home as well but failed to gain entry. My skin crawled imagining how narrowly I escaped time and again. At trial, dozens of victims described the psychological and physical devastation of being preyed upon in their sleep. My testimony was met with condescending disbelief until I defiantly lifted my shirt to show the jury my bruises. The orderly was swiftly sentenced to life behind bars for his years of exploiting vulnerable, sedated women.

His smug smirk faded as he was led away in cuffs. A tiny weight lifted from my weary spirit. But profound wounds remained. Trust, security, bodily autonomy - so much had been taken that could never be restored. When night came, I still double-checked locks and slept upright clutching a bat. Seeking any glimpse of healing, I joined a support group for others abused in clinical trials. Their haunted eyes and trauma mirrors reflected my own. Together we navigated the long road to reclaim our lives. I still walk this journey today. Police vigilance and time dull his trespasses somewhat, but the imprint on my cells remains.

My body has not forgotten, even if my mind tries desperately to do so. Some days this burden feels too heavy to bear. But I force myself to rise, nonetheless. To live boldly, angrily, beautifully. That is how I resist allowing his evil to spread further inside me. How I deny him his final stolen prize - my spirit. So, I lift my chin against the memories. I look towards the light until the shadows recede. And I refuse to be labeled a victim - because I alone define who I am, who I become. That power can never be taken without my consent again. I reclaimed myself once on my own terms, helping ensnare the monster haunting so many. I know, deep and weary in my bones, that I am brave and unbroken. And it is enough. It must be.

CHAPTER 9

TWO DATES

I SHOULD HAVE KNOWN from the first bumble date that Andre was bad news. The chemistry just wasn't there for me, but he seemed convinced we were soul-mates after one lukewarm coffee date. Still, I agreed to a second date against my better judgment. I figured I owed it to him to be sure there was no spark before calling it off. My instincts were right though. During date two, as Andre droned on about himself, I felt my energy being sapped. I hid yawns behind my hand and glanced at the door, eager for escape. Later that night, I texted him gently but firmly:

> You seem like a nice guy, but I didn't feel a romantic connection. Best of luck out there.

Short, polite, unambiguous.

I put Andre out of my mind and went back to my usual routine - working long bartending shifts, going out with friends, enjoying my independence. Two months passed without incident. Then the calls started. At first Andre was polite, asking for another chance, insisting we had "a deeper soul bond." I let the calls go to voicemail, tired but hoping he would get the hint. He didn't. The messages became more frequent, then almost daily. When I didn't return his calls, he became angry, accusing me of misleading him. I started to worry, but blocked his number and hoped that would be the end of it. It wasn't. A few nights later, I was working a crowded happy hour shift when the bar door slammed open.

My head jerked up to see Andre storming towards me, face contorted in rage. My heart dropped.

"There's my soulmate playing hard to get!" he shouted angrily over the music. "I know you feel this connection, don't deny it!"

Flustered, I stepped away from him. "Andre, leave now before I call security."

He banged his fist on the bar, causing patrons to jump. "Don't pretend you're too good for me, you whore!" he spat viciously. "No man wants a stuck-up slut like you anyway!"

I recoiled, shock shifting to anger. "That's it. Mike, get this scumbag out of here!" I shouted to the bouncer.

Before Andre could react, Mike grabbed him and hauled him towards the exit.

"You can't refuse a high value man like me!" Andre screamed desperately as he was dragged out. "I deserve you; you bitch!"

The door slammed shut behind him, cutting off his vile remarks. My hands were shaking as I turned back to my wide-eyed customers. "Sorry about that, folks. Drinks are on the house for the next fifteen!" I called out, attempting to diffuse the tension.

Mike came over after tossing Andre out on his ass. "You alright, Sam?" he asked gruffly.

I nodded, still rattled.

"That guy's bad news," Mike said. "I'll make sure he's banned from coming back."

I thanked Mike, hoping this would be the end of things. But over the next week, an unsettled feeling gnawed at me. The bar kept an eye out, but I never knew if Andre was waiting for me outside after my shifts. I took Ubers home from work each night rather than walking. One evening, I left through the back exit and cut down an alley to the nearby parking garage. As I rounded a corner, I heard loud footsteps behind me. Before I could react, someone grabbed my arm and spun me around. It was Andre.

"Hey baby, sneaking out the back for me?" he said, a dangerous glint in his eye.

I screamed and twisted away, adrenaline flooding my veins. Andre tried to grab me again, but I broke free and ran full speed toward the garage, his shouts echoing after me. I didn't slow down until I was locked inside my car, breathless and trembling all over. Peering into the shadows around the garage, I didn't see Andre anywhere. But I knew he was escalating. Over the next week, I called out of work several times, afraid he would be waiting for me again outside the bar. I only felt safe going between my apartment and car, constantly checking over my shoulder. Andre had staked himself outside my place of work, but I dreaded the thought of him tracking down my home address. The police couldn't do much without evidence of a direct threat. And with each passing day, the walls of my world narrowed. I jumped at every noise; terrified Andre was skulking in the shadows. I knew I needed to take real action soon, but uncertainty paralyzed me. For now, all I could do was go through the motions day by day, trying to hide my growing dread. I hoped against all reason that Andre would lose interest and this nightmare would end on its own. But in my gut, I knew this was only the beginning. Something had to give...I just prayed it wouldn't be my grip on sanity.

After Andre showed up unhinged at my job, his harassment only escalated. Despite banning him from the bar, I knew he was still lurking, waiting for me to emerge after each shift. I started using the back exits and taking Ubers home, terrified he'd confront me outside again. It wasn't enough to deter him. Soon, harassing messages started flooding my phone from an array of newly created numbers and accounts. On Instagram, Facebook, even random gaming platforms, vile messages appeared:

I'm always watching you

and

Don't ignore me bitch.

He must have paid services to track down all my accounts. I blocked each new profile, but Andre always found a way back in. His unhinged excuses gave way to threats, promising I'd regret brushing him off. The onslaught was endless. Exhausted and anxious, I barely ate or slept, dreading the next chilling message. I couldn't prove it was Andre behind them, but I knew.

One morning, an ominous email appeared with an attachment. Hands shaking, I opened it. Inside photos of my house from various angles, all taken at night from right outside the property.

The message read:

"I know where you live. Let me in."

Raw panic propelled me out of my chair. I ran through the house checking windows and doors, terrified Andre was already inside. But the place was empty. Still trembling, I called the police and filed for a restraining order. The court approved it right away, but Andre evaded the servers attempting to issue it.

Can't catch me, bitch!

A text taunted alongside a photo giving the camera the middle finger. The police said they needed to officially serve Andre before making an arrest. Meanwhile, the torment continued. I hardly went out anymore, jumping at every odd sound and passing car, certain Andre was closing in. I called out of my bartending shifts repeatedly; afraid he'd be lying in wait in the shadows nearby. Soon after, enraged emails from the bar's manager appeared, accusing me of flaking. I tried explaining the situation, but Andre had already poisoned them against me.

Less than a week later, I was fired. Even with a restraining order, the law couldn't shield me from Andre's omnipresent sabotage. His grudge consumed my every waking moment, destroying any sense of normalcy and security. Increasingly desperate, I used social media to spread the word about Andre's harassment campaign. I implored mutual connections to help me locate him so he could be served. Andre retaliated by anonymously sending my address, phone number, and workplace to shady forums rife with violent incels.

"Teach this uppity bitch a lesson," the posts said.

Soon, a whole new wave of violent threats flooded in from strangers. I shut down my social media presence, but it was too late to stop the spread of my personal information. Andre had successfully made me a target.

The police advised me to leave town for a while until they tracked Andre down. But I refused to be driven from my home like a fugitive. Nowhere felt safe but giving in to fear meant he won. My mistrust grew into paranoia. I isolated myself, questioning if anyone trying to befriend me was sent by Andre. I spent weekends barricaded alone indoors with the lights off, sobbing into a wine bottle. Somewhere along the way, stoic independence gave way to a creeping sense of inevitability. Andre had demolished the barriers between my world and his twisted fixation. Try as I might to block him out, he saturated every dark corner. Exhausted, hunted, and hollow, I prayed for the silent phone to herald the end of this nightmare. But its incessant buzzing never ceased. Eyes bloodshot from lack of sleep, I stared at the blank walls of my self-imposed prison. Andre was always circling, but the tighter I locked down, the closer he seemed to creep. This had to end before I lost my grip on reality entirely. But the light at the tunnel's end had never seemed so dim.

After losing my bartending job, I stayed with a friend briefly until I found a new job as a front desk clerk at a hotel downtown. I hoped working someplace secure like a hotel would provide a haven from Andre's torment. On my first week at the new job, the front door swung open and I looked up from the computer to see Andre strolling towards the front desk, red roses in hand. My blood turned to ice in my veins.

"Hey baby, brought you flowers for our first day back together," he said with a chilling smile.

My hands shaking, I threatened to call security.

Andre merely laughed. "You can't escape me that easily. I'll always find you, no matter where you hide."

To my dismay, he was right. Over the next few days, he called the hotel phone lines relentlessly, tying them up for hours at a time. When I begged my manager not to fire me, she just shook her head.

"We can't function like this. You're still in your probation period, I must let you go."

Again unemployed, I fell into a frantic search for work, any work, to pay my bills. But Andre sabotaged every new job within weeks, ensuring I'd be dismissed. He sent photos mocking my endless failed attempts to find security. All the while, I filed countless police reports. But Andre always slipped away before they could catch up to him, aided by his network of toxic contacts. When he got word I had reported him again, degrading messages would appear in my inbox:

"Stupid bitch, you can't stop me by whining to the cops."

The police assured me they were working hard to track him down. But Andre was always a ghost, vanishing before their grasp. Exhausted and hopeless, I sank into despair. Eviction notices piled up as I fell behind on rent. I drained my accounts on motels just to avoid sleeping in the home Andre had staked out. But money dwindled fast, and he tracked me down every time. Out of options, I listened to the police and moved clear across the state one last time.

But not one week passed before photos of my new front door appeared in my messages.

New place, same game.

The caption taunted. The walls closed in tighter. I saw Andre's face in crowds, imagined I heard his footsteps on quiet streets. When rare moments of sleep came, nightmares jolted me awake in a cold sweat. Friends tried to support me, but I pushed them away, crippled by paranoia that they were spies sent by Andre. No one could comprehend the hell that my life had become. More eviction warnings arrived, but I could barely get off the couch, much less find a job or home safe from his far reach. His siege had slowly severed me from any sense of normalcy.

In a last-ditch effort, I purchased a handgun and ammo for self-defense. The cold steel terrified me, but I forced myself to practice at the range daily until I could hit any target. My aim became lethally sharp, channeling all my rage and fear into each pull of the trigger. For the first time in ages, I felt a tiny spark of control. But even that wasn't enough to lift the smothering helplessness as the walls closed in. Sleepless and starved, I waited in the dark each night for the combat I knew was inevitable with Andre at this point. When a MySpace notification flashed on my old computer, I felt icy tendrils of dread uncoil. There was a new message from a blank profile with zero connections.

Of course, it was him. I opened it with trembling hands. Inside was a single picture - my new apartment complex, shot in the dead of night. The text below read:

I'm back, baby.

The last fragile thread of sanity holding me together finally snapped. All the fear and anguish twisted into steel-cold determination. The police couldn't catch him. I couldn't outrun him. There was only one way this ended... I loaded the pistol with steady hands. Eyes dark and clear, I waited for his inevitable return like a coiled snake ready to strike. The terror that had paralyzed me for so long crystallized into eerie calm. Whatever humanity or morality I clung to burned away, leaving only primal intent. He would never again breathe the same air, never violate the same space unchallenged. One way or another, by my own hands if necessary, this ended tonight. Finally, after all the humiliation and horror...I would be free.

For six harrowing months I waited, gun loaded, for Andre to make his final move. Most nights I slept upright on the couch, pistol nearby. The few times exhaustion overtook me in bed, I'd awaken to the jarring sounds of someone trying to break in - whether real or imagined, I never knew. Nearly every week, shouts and doorbell rings would shatter the silence as Andre made his presence known from outside, testing my endurance. But I held steady, jumping at shadows but refusing to abandon my post. One windy night, a different sound stirred me awake - the slow clicking and scraping of someone picking the front door lock.

In that split second, the months of fear crystallized into chilling purpose. Moving on instinct, I grabbed the pistol and took cover around the corner from the front hall, out of view of the door. With one hand I dialed 911, whispering desperately that an intruder was breaking in. The operator assured me police were on their way. The door creaked open, and I heard the distinct sound of Andre's heavy boots on the entryway floor. He was inside. The operator urged me to flee or hide, but my feet were rooted in place. The time for hiding was over. I peeked around the corner. A large silhouette slowly approached down the hall; the glint of a bat visible in his hands. My breath caught in my throat.

Just then, Andre turned and spotted me, his eyes going wide in surprise before a nasty grin spread across his face. "There you are, you heartless bitch," he growled, hefting the bat up. "Thought you could just cast me aside? I tried doing this the easy way, but you brought this on yourself." He advanced towards me; face twisted in malicious glee. "I'm going to enjoy beating some respect into you. Maybe after I'm done you won't be so stuck up. Hell, you may even learn to enjoy our special time together, once you know your place."

Despite the gun trembling in my hands, he kept coming, revolting threats spilling from his lips. I backward away from him down the hall, but he pursued like a predator corralling wounded prey.

"One way or another, you're going to be mine tonight," he declared.

At that, something defiant and feral erupted in me. I

planted my feet and aimed the pistol dead at his chest. "Come one step closer and I swear I'll shoot!" I shouted. "The police are already on their way. It's over, Andre!"

He paused for a second, then let out an eerie chuckle. "We both know you don't have the guts," he sneered. "Now be a good girl." He drew back the bat, readying a vicious swing.

In that heartbeat, the months of fear burning inside me ignited into blistering rage. As the bat whipped toward my head, I pulled the trigger. Once, twice, three shots in rapid succession. Two bullets ripped into Andre's abdomen.

He stumbled back with a scream, the bat dropping from his hands. For a long moment we stared at each other, both stunned by what just happened.

Then the distant sound of sirens pierced the silence. With an agonized howl, Andre turned and staggered out the front door, leaving a trail of blood in his wake. After he fled, I sank to my knees, numb with shock but finally free of the terror that had consumed me. By the time the police arrived, Andre had vanished into the night. But they quickly tracked him by following the blood trail a few blocks away to an alley where he had collapsed. He was rushed to emergency surgery under police watch. As soon as he was stable, Andre was arrested and charged with stalking, harassment, attempted murder, and breaking and entering. Meanwhile, I gave my eyewitness testimony about the night's events. The self-defense shooting was ruled legally justified given the circumstances, and no charges were filed against me. I never had to see Andre again.

He took a plea deal and is now serving out a lifetime sentence far away. The long nightmare that had upended my life finally came to an end. The trauma lingers, as I try to rebuild myself stronger than before. But Andre's shadow, once inescapable, fades more each day I breathe free air. I don't look over my shoulder anymore. The doors and windows stay open again. I reconnected with loved ones, returned to work, moved someplace warm and bright. There are still hard days, but also joyful moments that Andre could never steal again. In the end, he failed to extinguish my spirit and resolve. I survived his twisted obsession. And though healing is ongoing, the time has come to close this dark chapter for good. To let it become just one part of my greater story - not the ending. My ending has not yet been written.

CHAPTER 10

TWIN PEEKS

AS A YOUNG SINGLE WOMAN, I've had my fair share of bad dates. But this last guy Bob took clinginess to the extreme. After only two dates, he bombarded me with needy texts like:

> Why won't you see me anymore? You're such an ungrateful bitch!

I rolled my eyes at the unfair vitriol and blocked his number. I wasn't going to engage with some bitter dude bro's fragile ego. I've dealt with controlling creeps before. This was nothing new under the sun. Bob was just another drop in the bucket of weirdos I encountered in the dating pool. Brushing it off came easily after so much practice weeding through the frogs to find a prince. No point dwelling on one oddball's rude behavior. I had a fun girls' night to get ready for. My twin sister Lisa, on the other hand, seemed to be having the opposite dating luck lately. A secret admirer had been lavishing her with huge bouquets of roses and expensive jewelry over the past month. She was over the moon about her new mystery beau, though she couldn't figure out who he was yet.

At first, I was thrilled for her finally getting the fairy tale romance she always dreamed of. Lisa had the worst judgment in men, always falling for players. But maybe this anonymous romantic was a keeper. However, Lisa's euphoria soon morphed into unease. The extravagant gifts kept arriving like clockwork, observed by this mystery man but never with any note or outright reveal of his identity. It all felt a bit...excessive. Then odd incidents started occurring - her tires got slashed overnight, someone rifled through her garbage cans, the rose bouquets displayed on her porch suddenly appeared wilted and dead after days of blooming. Peculiar, but easy to write off as random misfortunes.

But Lisa couldn't ignore the escalating harassment at the daycare where she worked. Several times a week, an anonymous male caller would phone the daycare leaving disturbing messages. He claimed Lisa a "pedophile" and "sex worker" who should be kept far from children. Obviously, none of it was true, but Lisa was forced to take leave at the threat of losing her job if the inflammatory calls persisted. She was a total wreck, convinced a bitter ex was out to ruin her life even though she had no proof. I came over as soon as I got her desperate, sobbing phone call. Seeing my bold, vibrant sister curled up on her bed staring blankly left me shaken.

This campaign against her came out of nowhere, but clearly it was destroying her. As I hugged her tight and smoothed her hair, I assured her we'd get to the bottom of this harassment. Had she told anyone about the gifts from her secret admirer? Could this be some sick ploy to control her through terror? Lisa shook her head, equally puzzled. She hadn't told anyone except me about the gifts just in case it ruined a good thing. None of it made sense. All she knew was this phantom was hell-bent on upending her life for reasons she couldn't grasp. I held her as she cried herself to sleep, wishing I could spirit this torment away. But all I could do was be there as her pillar of support until we identified who was intent on bringing her so low, and why. Whatever dark fixation fueled this elaborate revenge scheme had only just begun...

The morning after I comforted Lisa, we decided to call into work. She was in no shape to handle a roomful of rambunctious kids, and I wanted to be with her. We needed a girls' day to unwind from the stress of her phantom tormentor. As we slipped our coffee, the dark circles under Lisa's eyes betrayed her lack of sleep.

But she gave me a timid smile. "Thanks for staying over. I really needed my twin last night."

I squeezed her hand supportively. We were going to get through this together. I suggested a corny movie marathon with face masks and junk food to distract from her troubles. Lisa perked up at the idea. We spent the day giggling over rom-coms, painting each other's nails, and gossiping like old times. For a few blissful hours, the harassment faded into the background. Lisa's smile finally reached her eyes again. As the sky darkened, we settled in at the kitchen table over steaming plates of pasta. Lisa seemed more relaxed than she had in weeks.

Outside, rain pattered gently against the windows, the perfect background noise. Across from me, Lisa was recounting a silly story from work when suddenly she froze, fork halted mid-bite. Her face had gone sheet white. Before I could ask what was wrong, the window behind me exploded in a hail of glass. The deafening crack of multiple gunshots followed, barely drowned out by our screams. Lisa leapt up, pulling me to the floor and shielding my body with hers. More bullets zinged overhead, splintering chairs, and lodging in cabinets. We crawled desperately to take cover in the next room, broken glass biting my palms and knees. The gunfire seemed concentrated on the kitchen as we huddled together against the wall shaking. Finally, the barrage ceased, followed by shouting voices in the yard next door.

Lisa kept pressure on my bleeding shoulder - when had I been hit? - as we remained flattened on the floor awaiting the next round. Instead, blessed sirens soon screamed outside. We limped out the front door into the arms of police with their guns drawn, scouring for the shooter. An ambulance whisked me off to urgently treat and extract the bullet in my shoulder. Lisa refused to leave my side even for a second, her face etched with trauma and fury at the unknown assailant. As I was stabilized in the ER, she told detectives all about the horrific harassment escalating up to this moment. They assured armed officers would provide round-the-clock protection to us both until the shooter was caught. Lisa insisted we stay together at her place with the guard, terrified something fatal could happen to me if we separated. I didn't argue; the phantom's attacks had turned brazen and lethal.

Tonight, could have easily been our last if the bullet's aim had been just slightly different. We clung to each other, feeling like the only two people left in the world. Yet even the emergency responders' help began feeling out of reach. The stalker seemed to know no limits, able to invade any space or moment we dared believe was safe. Waiting on the floor that night with the darkness and silence amplified our hypervigilance. Each creak or rustle made us squeeze each other's hands tighter. Sleep was impossible. In the morning, numb resignation had replaced shocked disbelief. Someone truly wanted me dead, and they would stop at nothing until it was accomplished. Nowhere was safe - all we could do was huddle in terror and try to delay the inevitable. Because in my heart of hearts, I knew our stalker would not rest until my corpse lay at my sister's feet. This monster's appetite for pain and control would never be satisfied, even if it ended for one or both of us. Our only weapons now were buying time and staying together...even if, in the end, the faceless evil lurking in the shadows inevitably won.

The sound of nearby gunfire jolted us. Lisa and I clung together, breaths frozen, as shouts and bursts of shooting erupted right outside. This was it - the stalker was making his final move. Lisa's eyes rolled back as she slipped into unconsciousness from fear. I tried shaking her but couldn't tear my own petrified gaze from the kitchen door, certain it would burst open to reveal our crazed assassin. But instead, the booming shots gradually died down, replaced by running feet and police radios crackling. An officer shouted our names - help had arrived.

As they broke down the front door, I flagged medics over to the limp form of my sister. EMTs quickly loaded me onto a stretcher while officers escorted Lisa outside to an ambulance. We were sped off under blaring sirens to the hospital, the flashing lights illuminating the eerie, down-pouring night. At the hospital, I demanded updates on Lisa while a doctor treated my own shock symptoms and blood pressure spike. Mercifully, he soon returned to confirm Lisa had simply fainted from terror but was awake now and asking for me. I ran to Lisa's room, and we embraced tearfully, neither quite believing we had survived another attack by our unrelenting stalker.

Officer escorts arrived to keep guard over us both as we underwent tests. Sometime later, two detectives entered our room, their expressions grim. Lisa and I looked at each other anxiously - had the shooter gotten away? But no, they informed us he had died during the standoff outside Lisa's home. In horrified disbelief, we listened as they outlined the discoveries made about this man who had nearly taken our lives. He had left behind a diary and manifesto detailing his obsession. Apparently he was a rejected suitor, Bob, from my past who thought he saw me one day outside the grocery store. But it must have been Lisa, my identical twin. In his warped mind though, I was just playing hard to get.

Enraged by this perceived heartbreak, the man fixated on Lisa as a representation of me. He followed her, vandalized her property, made harassing calls to her work. When she continued seeming happy despite his terror campaign, his hand was forced - she had to die.

The detectives looked disgusted as they summarized the unhinged rantings and plotting this monster had meticulously recorded to get back at me through my oblivious sister. Lisa and I stared hollowly ahead, overwhelmed by the meaningless tragedy of it all. In the end, taking Lisa's life was just part of this madman's grand plan to go out in a blaze of glory while devastating the woman who rejected him. We had been nothing but props in his self-centered spectacle of violence.

The unfairness stung bitterly. Our statements given, Lisa and I sat wrecked in the sterile hospital room trying to process the revelations. Our lives had been parasitic collateral damage for some lone creep's crusade of outrage against the world. It felt so senselessly violating. As we made tentative plans to visit a beach cottage to recuperate when released from the hospital, tears flowed again at how close we had come to being two more bodies left behind by an unhinged misogynist. The doctors monitored us both for symptoms of lasting trauma from repeated terror. But having each other kept us grounded through the darkest moments. Comforted that the phantom was gone for good, we chose to focus on healing. The long process of reclaiming security lies ahead, but side by side, I know Lisa and I will persevere. The cruelty of strangers shook us profoundly, but our love never wavered. And that light can outshine any darkness if you let it.

CHAPTER 11

PIZZA PANIC

AS A PIZZA CHEF at Tony's Pizzeria, I loved whipping up made-to-order pies in our open kitchen. Customers could sit at the counter and watch us work like a show. I took pride in spinning dough, ladling sauces, and of course, dramatic oven reveals. A good pizza night kept me in flow state for hours. It was a typical busy Tuesday dinner rush. My hands were flying, stretching, and topping pies before sliding them into the blazing brick oven. I called out names as piping hot pizzas emerged, keeping the orders moving. Between pies, I noticed a man sitting alone at the counter just... watching me. He didn't have a ticket or drink. Figuring he was just waiting to order; I didn't think much of it. The oven didn't pause for gawkers. After the rush passed, I cleaned up my station and approached him to take his order.

"Hey there, welcome to Tony's! Have you been helped yet?"

The man just smiled and said nope, he was still thinking about it.

When I asked what he'd like, he requested I make my favorite pizza. Caught off guard, I laughed and told him the Margherita was my go-to. I freshly rolled out the dough and assembled the classic combo of sauce, fresh mozzarella, and basil. As I worked, the stranger watched my every move intently. I chalked it up to curiosity and slid the finished pie into the oven. When it emerged bubbling hot, I served him with a smile. He thanked me and dug in, never taking his eyes off me. After he left, I put the odd encounter out of mind. Just an indecisive customer.

But the next Tuesday, the man was back in the same spot at the counter, just watching me work. After an hour, he called me over and requested "my specialty" again. I hid my unease behind a customer service smile and put in the Margherita. This became a pattern week after week - the man would sit, observe me, then order the same pizza I made that first night. My coworkers thought it was a little weird, but harmless enough. Still, I felt increasingly uncomfortable under his gaze. One busy Friday, the familiar man claimed his usual counter seat. After an hour of staring, he asked for a Margherita pizza...and my phone number written on the box. Laughing nervously, I declined and put in his order quickly.

After that, he started placing takeout orders for delivery and requesting I personally prepare it. The orders came daily, always watching me work first. My boss just saw it as good business, but my skin crawled. Approaching the counter made me anxious now. The man – James, I overheard from another server – would just smile and stare. No matter how busy I looked, he waited for my undivided attention. The flattering intrigue I first felt morphed into tension knotting my shoulders whenever James lurked around. I no longer found making his lunchtime pizza fun or inspiring. But I had bills to pay, so I forced uneasy smiles and cooked on. The only saving grace was the counter separating me from his unrelenting gaze. At least while at work, I had that barrier. What he did outside those doors was out of my hands. And the thought filled me with creeping unease I couldn't shake.

After I rejected giving James my number, he surprisingly backed off coming into Tony's as often. He'd still lurk outside or order for delivery, but the uncomfortable staring sessions at the counter ceased. I was relieved he seemed to finally respect my boundaries. The pizzeria went back to feeling like my fun, safe haven from the world's problems. On a slow, snowy January night, I got roped into helping deliver pies since business was slow. I bundled up and grabbed a stack of orders to load into my car. Glancing at the receipts, I saw a familiar name – James had ordered delivery tonight.

My stomach knotted, but at least I wouldn't have to see him in person at the house. I pulled up the long, winding driveway he had given as the address. The isolated house loomed out of the darkness, not another neighbor in sight. The unease prickled, but I shook it off. Just another delivery, I told myself.

James was already waiting at the door when I got out of the car, pizza in hand. "Wow, great service, you brought it yourself!" he said with an unsettling grin.

I avoided his eyes and double-checked the receipt. "Yep, cash payment due on this one," I said briskly. But when I looked up, James had already gone back inside, leaving the door ajar.

He called out for me to come in out of the cold while he grabbed his wallet. I hesitated on the doorstep, alarm bells ringing distantly in my mind. But the freezing wind decided for me. I stepped inside and shut the door. The house looked tidy and conventional – not at all the deranged lair I irrationally feared. No sign of kids or a family like James had mentioned. But I forced a smile, ready to get paid and get out. As James rummaged around for his wallet, he told me sit down and stay a while since I had come all this way. We should enjoy my specialty pizza together. My eyes flitted to the front door – and my heart dropped to see the deadbolt locked from the inside.

Fear flooded my veins. I had made a grave mistake coming inside. I stammered excuses about needing to get back to work and tried to unlock the doorknob. But suddenly, a heavy bottle struck the back of my head, exploding in pain and bright flashes. Dazed, I collapsed to the floor. Through the ringing in my ears, I heard James apologize – said he had tried asking nicely so many times. But I left him no choice. We clearly belonged together. My vision swam as he leaned over me, caressing my face. I tried pushing his hands away weakly as he began tugging at my work uniform. Fear jolted me alert despite the throbbing agony in my skull. Adrenaline flooded my muscles and I lashed out, scratching and kicking viciously.

James just chuckled, aroused by my struggle. "I love it when they fight back," he growled in my ear. His fingers wrapped around my throat, cutting off my screams. As darkness crept in at the edges of my vision, my hands scrambled desperately across the floor, searching for anything to defend myself.

Dazed from the wine bottle blow, I desperately swept

my hands across the floor for anything to defend myself as James pinned me down. My fingers closed around the bottle's neck, jagged from breaking. With all the strength I had left, I gripped the fractured glass and swung with primal urgency. It plunged into James' stomach. He howled in shock and rage, loosening his hold just enough for me to wrench free. I bolted for the back of the house on pure adrenaline, weaving and stumbling. In my blurry state, I raced past a dining room wallpapered with photos of me at work. Revulsion scorched through me at the evidence of his twisted obsession. Just ahead I spotted the back door and made straight for it, fumbling to unlock it before James could grab me again. My hands slick with blood left crimson smears on the door as I desperately twisted the lock. Finally, it clicked open, and I burst outside into the stinging, snowy darkness. The icy air shocked my system, but my legs kept pumping. I had to get as far from that house of horrors as possible. In my panicked state, I didn't even think to grab my keys or phone. The dark forest surrounding the property seemed my only chance to escape, so I plunged into the black woods.

The freezing ground bit my socked feet as I fled blindly between the trees. Beating back brambles and stumbling over roots, only one thought compelled me forward – get away. After what felt like an eternity, I broke through the tree line and spotted in the distance a tiny cabin with a light glowing inside. With my last ounce of strength, I staggered to the door and pounded desperately, praying help was within. A startled older woman answered and pulled me inside without hesitation when she saw my bedraggled state. In the safety and warmth of her living room, the adrenaline wore off. I dissolved into heaving sobs as she wrapped a blanket around me and called the police. Soon red and blue lights flashed outside the cabin windows.

I recounted in fragments to the officers what James had done to me back at the house. They had an ambulance take me to the hospital to assess my head injury. There, they informed me James had been found unconscious in a crashed car a mile from his home. The stab wound I inflicted appeared to have made him lose control of the vehicle as he gave pursuit down the isolated road. My stomach turned, imagining what horrors might have awaited me had I not made it to the sanctuary of the woods. James was rushed into emergency surgery under police guard to remove his spleen and repair intestinal damage. According to officers, while raiding James' home they uncovered disturbing evidence of his fixation – photos, clothing items, a diary detailing his imagined plans for us. My skin crawled at how close I came to being another "beloved" prisoner locked in his fantasy.

My concussion and lacerations were minor compared

to what James intended to inflict on me in that house. But the trauma of fighting for my life against a delusional madman would leave scars far deeper than surface wounds. In the weeks that followed, vivid flashbacks ambushed me without warning. I jumped at every unexpected sound, once even punching a coworker who startled me. Sleep brought only nightmares ending with my bloody death. Plainly, I could no longer safely work in such a public, hectic environment as a pizzeria. With a heavy heart, I was forced to resign from my beloved job. The city also carried too many haunting reminders, so I relocated to a rural town hours away. My new job was solitary and mundane - customer service calls from home for a faceless corporation. But it paid bills while I underwent intensive trauma therapy. Years later, my jumpiness diminished along with the frequency of the flashbacks.

James is serving a lifetime sentence. I reunited with passionate cooking through weekend catering gigs. But that ravenous look in James' eye as he attacked burns in my memory as permanently as the photos of me papering his sick shrine. No amount of time or distance heals such violation completely. You learn to live with the shadow it casts. I still feel uneasy passing isolated homes at night or seeing someone watch me too intently from across a room. But I refuse to live in fear. Now I listen to my inner voice when intuition whispers, I am not safe. That is the lesson hardship taught me. Though innocence was lost that night in the darkness, strength emerged forged in its flames. I survived evil's best efforts to consume me. And my spirit still rises boldly from the ashes, tempered by fire into courage wielded as my shield. No longer naïve prey - a fighter who trusts her instincts, meets darkness unflinching, and claims joy defiantly. This is the phoenix reborn.

———

CONTINUE WITH
STALKED: VOLUME 4

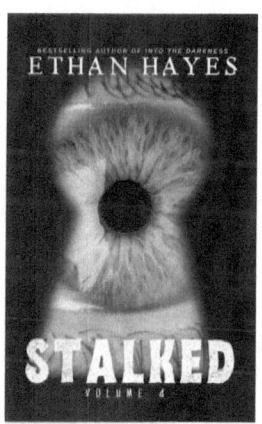

OR GRAB ETHAN HAYES'S CHILLING SERIES
TALES OF TERROR

OR READ ONE OF FREE REIGN PUBLISHING'S
OTHER AUTHORS

ABOUT THE AUTHOR

Ethan Hayes grew up in Oklahoma and moved to Texas when he attended Texas A&M. Upon graduation he was hired by Texas Parks and Wildlife and remained there until he retired twenty-two years later. He currently lives in southeast Texas with his wife and two dogs. When he's not spending time enjoying the outdoors and writing, he sips a cold beer on his front porch while listening to Bluegrass music.

———

Send in your encounter story:
encountersbigfoot@gmail.com

ALSO BY ETHAN HAYES

ALSO BY FREE REIGN PUBLISHING